To: Bev
Merry Christmas!
Beth

Driftwood

D1738018

by
Beth Mitchum

Embrace transformation!

Beth A. Mitchum

Windstorm Creative Limited
Port Orchard, WA

Driftwood
copyright © 2000 by Beth Mitchum
published by Windstorm Creative Limited

ISBN 1-883573-19-X

9 8 7 6 5 4 3 2
First Edition October 2000

Cover Design by CKD for Blue Artisans
Interior Design by CKD for Blue Artisans
Series Design by Windstorm Creative
Edited by Natalie Brown
Cover Photo by Robin Houpt

This is a work of fiction. Any resemblance to persons living or dead is coincidental.

Windstorm Creative Limited is a six imprint, international organization involved in publishing books in all genres, including electronic publications; producing games, toys, videos and audio cassettes as well as producing theatre, film and visual arts events.

Windstorm Creative Limited
7419 Ebbert Drive Southeast
Port Orchard WA 98367
360-769-7174
driftwood@windstormcreative.com
www.windstormcreative.com

Acknowledgements

First of all, I'd like to thank Jennifer DiMarco for reading my manuscript for fun. I'm glad you liked it enough to pass it on to Cris and Natalie. I'm really glad all of you enjoyed it enough to want to publish it. My thanks to Cris Newport and Natalie Brown for their editorial contributions. I would also like to thank the many friends who were my readers for earlier versions of this book, particularly Jean Stewart, whose timely words helped immensely.

Of course, I need to thank Robin for putting up with me when I was in that creative trance. I know you thought that I would never eat if you didn't' bring me food, but I really would've come up for sustenance at some point. I just wouldn't have eaten anything as healthy and delicious as what you served me.

Thanks, too, to my four furry feline fellows. You kept my lap warm in the winter while I was madly typing on my keyboard. Your love and companionship is a blessing. I apologize of I was overly distracted when you wanted me to play.

Last, but definitely not least, thanks to my mom for being the coolest mom on the planet. You've always been my most staunch supporter in all my endeavors. Oh, yeah, I guess that's because you're my mother.

Driftwood

by
Beth Mitchum

Windstorm Creative Limited
Port Orchard, WA

Dedication

To Robin.

Chapter 1

I knew from the moment I spotted her on the beach that my life would never be the same. I don't know what it was exactly that drew my attention to her. Yet I knew instinctively that she was it—the catalyst. I was forever changed before the first "hello."

I had just finished washing the dishes in my cottage on the Oregon coast. It was September, and my husband and I were taking the first vacation he had managed to steal away from his interminable caseload. Paul was a successful lawyer. I was his wife. I had been begging him all year to take me to the beach for a change of scenery. Out of self-preservation, he finally arranged it. He had tried initially to convince me to go by myself, but I refused. I wanted my husband by my side. I didn't want to travel alone, like a woman who didn't have a man who cared for her. It wasn't long, however, before I began wishing I had left him behind.

It was on the evening of the second day of our vacation that I found myself walking alone on the beach. The summer crowds had dwindled away, so I was able to amble along without running into more than a dozen people. I assumed that these were mostly local residents, with perhaps a few visitors taking advantage of the off-season to spend a peaceful week at Cannon Beach.

As I walked on the loose sand, my gaze took in the waves crashing against the dark rocks that lay scattered along the shore. Huge rocks that reminded me of giant toys left behind by titanic gods of another world. Their size amazed me. Their geologic history intrigued me. As I surveyed the scene, it was hard to tell which was the stronger of the two elements. I knew that water had the ability to wear away the hard, solid surface. Yet as the powerful waves slammed into the rocks, they were instantly transformed into mere saline droplets. Watching this interplay of water and rock, I felt as though the rocks were my heart, and the waves my emotions. Feeling a slight chill in these thoughts, I pulled my windbreaker close around me, as I walked in the direction of Haystack Rock, the largest remnant of volcanic expulsions found at this particular point along the shore.

I came upon her at a particularly isolated section of the beach. She was sitting atop one of the many logs that had washed up on the shore. She herself looked nearly as weathered and battered as the wood upon which she was perched. Her long indigo hair was flipping wildly in the ocean breeze, snaking around the acoustic guitar that was cradled in her arms. She was wearing a navy blue T-shirt and a pair of faded and tattered blue jeans. Her feet were bare, although I noticed an incongruently new pair of blue Birkenstock sandals next to where she was seated.

It was her silhouette that first caught my attention. She was playing her guitar and singing passionately to the waves, though I could hear nothing but the sound of the wind and the crashing waves in my ears. Desiring to hear her voice, I ventured closer, hoping she wouldn't stop her performance before I could get near enough to hear what she was singing. I approached from the rear, for I had the distinct impression that she wouldn't appreciate having an audience.

When I got within hearing range I was delighted to find that her voice was rich and mellow, like a vintage red wine, smooth and silky, and just a tad sweet. I inhaled the melodic bouquet, swishing the sounds around in my head. Her guitar sounded full and sensuous, it's tones creating resonance with the emotions in my heart. By the time she finished her song, I was close enough to reach out and touch her; but I didn't. Instead I waited breathlessly for the music to begin again. When it did, I eased myself into a sitting position on a nearby log.

I had seated myself just to the right of her. Hopefully far enough behind her that she wouldn't notice me, yet close enough to watch her marvelously talented hands. She was playing an intricate tune on her guitar, her trained fingers finding just the right spots on the neck of her instrument. Her right hand deftly picking out the melody in a way that made me feel as though she were making love to her guitar, rather than merely playing it. I strained to understand the words that were falling from her lips.

> Things have changed; I've lost my way.
> The skies I used to see have faded into gray.
> Day by day, I've fallen back.
> Memories of my yesteryear have thrown me off
>   the track.

> Looking ahead to the morning sun.
> Trying to stop myself from being on the run.
> Life is not as I wanted it to be.
> I've become someone who is not really me.

> Choices are simple, as long as they're not mine.
> Answers are easy, but changing takes up time.
> I can never face tomorrow from the standpoint
>   of today.
> Goals I want to reach are a million miles away.

> Letting go of the days gone by.
> Praying that the veil will fall from my eyes.
> I'm going to find that road again.
> It may take time and just a little bit of pain.

> Choices are simple, as long as they're not mine.
> Answers are easy, but changing takes up time.
> I can never face tomorrow from the standpoint
>   of today.
> Goals I want to reach, they are a million miles away.

She followed a passionate repetition of the chorus with more instrumentation, then turned her head to look at me. She gave me a polite, and somewhat shy, smile. Her eyes were guarded, as though she were unsure what to do next. I half expected her to get up and walk away; but she didn't. Instead she just turned her gaze back upon the ocean while she sat there hugging her guitar. Then she turned back towards me and said, "You live around here?"

Her speaking voice was nearly as rich and hypnotic as her singing voice. After having been silent for so long, I managed to whisper hoarsely, "I, no, I don't . . .." As my voice warmed to the task of communicating, I managed to continue in a normal tone, "Well, actually I do own a house here, but I don't get to come very often."

She started to smile, but instead knitted her brows and said, "Where do you normally live?"

"Portland. My husband and I are on vacation."

From the moment the words escaped my lips, I knew I had said something that displeased her. I searched my mind trying to figure out what it was that had painted such a disappointed look on her face. Was it that I was on vacation? Was it that I was from Portland? What was she thinking?

All she said was, "Oh, I see." Then she turned away from me to look out towards the horizon again, as though she had ended the conversation, and was letting me know that I was free to go at any time.

"Do you?" I asked quietly, half to myself, not expecting her to hear my words.

She looked back at me with a puzzled expression. "Do I what?"

I stood up to leave, but decided to repeat the question, since she had asked. I looked directly into her eyes. "Do you see?"

She gave her head a brief shake. "I think you lost me there." She looked at me with curiosity, as though I were a quaint little circus sideshow few people would pay to see.

I turned my gaze towards the ocean, trying to avoid her bemused look. "I told you I was from Portland, and that my husband and I were vacationing here. Then you said, 'Oh, I see,' as though you had concluded something about me from that information. I just wondered what it was you had decided about me."

She shrugged, then raised one hand in bewilderment. "I think I was just trying to be polite. I don't go in for small talk much, so you'll have to excuse me."

I laughed at the look of discomfort on her face. "I'm sorry. I'm behaving rather oddly, aren't I? I didn't mean to make you feel uncomfortable. I was just curious about what you meant by 'Oh, I see.' Call me vain, if you will, but I wanted to know what it was you were envisioning. Were you really learning something about me? Were you finding hidden meaning in my words? Never mind. I don't have the foggiest idea what's come over me. I'm not usually like this. Really."

"Not a problem." She got up and slipped her sandals on, as though she were about to leave.

"Don't go!"

She frowned at me and cocked her head to one side. "Are you all right? Do you need help? I mean, do you need someone to talk to or something?"

"No! I mean, yes, I'm all right. No, I don't need anyone to talk to." I paused, and took stock of the thoughts and emotions that were violently colliding inside me, then said, "Well, yes, perhaps I do need someone to talk to. Do you have a minute? I could buy you a latte, if you'd like."

She smiled at me and shook her head. "I'll pass on the latte. I'd be up all night if I drank one now."

"Okay, so how about some frozen yogurt?"

She laughed. "Okay, frozen yogurt it is." Using the strap that was attached to it, she slung her guitar onto her back, and gestured for me to lead the way.

I leaped up, brushed the sand from my knit slacks, and headed up the beach towards town. I waited for her to catch up with me, so we could walk side by side. "I suppose you think I'm completely insane by now. I'm not usually like this. I didn't think I needed to talk to anyone. Then suddenly I realized that was exactly what I needed."

"And who better to talk to than a stranger playing her guitar on the beach, right?"

"I hadn't really thought about it in that way. Am I being pushy? I'm playing this by ear, so to speak. I saw you out there on the log, and I felt compelled to get close enough to hear you.   I just knew you must have a magnificent alto voice."

She smiled at me and shook her head again. "Sorry if I disappointed you."

"What disappointment? You do have a magnificent voice! It's sounds just as I expected, perhaps a little better even."

"Thanks."

"Have you been playing long?"

"About twenty years now."

"Heavens! How old are you?"

"Thirty-three, I think."

"You don't know?"

"I don't pay much attention to time. What year is this? 1995, right?"

I nodded, so she continued. "Then yes, I'm thirty-three, and I've been playing and singing for twenty years now."

"Gracious.   I can't imagine doing anything for twenty years."

"Not even being married?" Her nonchalant glance was like a blow to the side of my brain. I stopped walking and looked at her intently. "What an odd question."

She stopped walking too, stuffed one hand in the pocket of her jeans and looked down at the sand, as though trying to avoid my gaze. "Sorry. I say odd things sometimes."

I looked down at her feet. She was lazily etching an arc in the sand with her right foot. It looked to me like a smile, a mocking smile. "I don't know that I can imagine being married for twenty years, now that you mention it."

Her gaze returned to my face. "How long have you been married?"

"Fifteen years this past June."

She smiled somewhat ruefully at me. "Then you'd better start figuring out what you'd rather be doing, because you're running out of time."

I shook my head, and stared at her even more intently. "You're making my head hurt."

She laughed a bit, then said, "Sorry. I've been known to do that to people."

"Make their heads hurt?"

She nodded. "I'm sorry if I've upset you. I don't try to do it. It just sort of happens. I listen to what people say, try to hear the meaning behind their words, then respond. Somehow that comes out in a way that makes people uncomfortable. It isn't a conscious thing. I don't think I could do it if I were consciously trying. I just state what I perceive to be the obvious. Only it usually isn't all that obvious to anyone else."

I turned and looked back at the ocean. "But you're right. I've never really thought about it before, but I can't imagine being married to Paul for twenty years. Yet it has almost happened without my being aware of it."

She shrugged. "Time gets away from us all."

"Yes," I said sadly, "I suppose it does."

We started walking again towards the ice cream shop. I couldn't put the thought out of my head that I had been married for over fifteen years. The worst part was that I really didn't like the idea of being married to Paul for that long. It wasn't that the reality of it was so bad. We got along well enough. Too well really. We seldom fought, which I sometimes viewed as being an indication that we had a good relationship. In my rare moments of dissatisfaction, however, I knew that we seldom fought because we seldom saw each other. He was always at work. I was always making the social rounds, playing the part of the politically correct wife who was saving the world through her volunteer work. Most of the time, Paul and I were little more than roommates.

"Are you married?" I asked abruptly.

She laughed and shook her head, her eyes dancing with mischief. "Oh no. They don't let my kind marry, and I wouldn't marry if they did."

"What do you mean, 'your kind?'"

"Lesbians. We're not allowed to get married legally. Sure, we can have some sort of religious ceremony if we know a sympathetic pastor, but we haven't yet been given the privilege of legal matrimony. That's one of the 'special rights' political conservatives are paranoid about granting to us. They're afraid we'll poison society with our perverted love." She rolled her eyes in derision, then looked at me from the side to see how I was taking this information.

"I see."

She laughed. "That's fair enough. I've just given you my first self-revelatory remark, and you gave me the same response I gave you. The summing up of an entire life, filled with complications and intricacies, into a single stereotype—lesbian separatist. If we're going to sit down and have a heart to heart talk, then I should confess that I was probably writing you off as a yuppie heterosexist woman who lives to please men. An unfair judgment, no doubt, but it's really difficult when you first meet someone. Humans seem to have a terrible need to categorize everything. You say one thing to me about who you are, I automatically stick you in the yuppie het woman slot, and dismiss you as uninteresting."

"Your honesty is rather unnerving. Are you always this candid, or did my blithering introduction set the pace for the rest of this conversation?"

"I'm usually this honest, though I have to admit that your initial response to my cursory dismissal immediately removed you from the 'uninteresting' category."

"So how do I get out of the heterosexist category? I consider myself heterosexual, but not heterosexist."

She smiled at me and looked me boldly in the eyes. "Let me kiss you right here in public."

"What?!?"

She bent over laughing, trying hard to keep her guitar strap from slipping off her shoulder. "That was a joke. I'm sorry. I couldn't resist."

I tried to act as though this woman weren't making me feel terribly uncomfortable. "You know, you don't look like a lesbian separatist."

"No? What does one look like then?"

"Most of the ones I've known have really short haircuts and multiple body piercings."

"Yeah, well, me too, but I'm not actually a separatist. That was just the label I figured you would stick on me. I'm just a lesbian who likes to stay separate from everyone, not just men. I personally don't give a fig that gays can't get married, because I'd never want to lie to myself, or my lover. I don't feel that it's honest for me to take vows of 'until death do us part.' How can I know whether I will love the same person twenty years from now? I don't even know where I'll be two months from now. I may be backpacking across Europe or kayaking along the Alaskan coast. How can I say 'I'll stay beside you forever and always?'"

"But couldn't you do those things with someone else?"

"I don't know. It's not that I don't ever have a lover, or that I don't ever have a traveling companion. It's just that it isn't usually the same person year after year. Relationships bottom out, and I'm ready to move on. There's too much to see in this world to get stuck in one place, working nine to five, day in and day out, just to make house payments."

"How do you live? What do you use for money?"

"I usually sleep in my truck. It has a camper on the back."

"You mean you're homeless?"

"Now don't look at me like that. And don't even think about making me into an object of pity. I'm not homeless. I just don't own a stationary home, and I seldom bother renting an apartment because they usually make you sign a lease. I don't like being tied down like that."

"A drifter."

Her blue eyes hardened to slate, as she looked at me.

"Yeah, okay, I'm a drifter. That's something you do by choice. Homeless people aren't usually homeless by choice. I am. I work for awhile in one town—doing odd jobs, waiting tables, playing gigs, if I'm lucky. Then I move on to another place I've always wanted to see."

"Like where?"

"Anywhere I haven't been."

"Isn't that dangerous?"

"Isn't what dangerous?"

"Living in your truck."

"Not any more than living in your house. I usually stop in a state park or private campground. Then I stay a few days, weeks, or several months, depending on whether I like the place. I'm safe enough. I'm not sleeping on the streets."

"What about showers?"

"Campgrounds usually have showers."

"Oh. Well, what about food?"

"What do you mean?"

"How do you eat?"

"With two hands, the same way I make love."

The look she gave me startled me. It was both seductive and innocently playful. I stopped walking again and turned to face her. "Are you trying to offend me?"

"Why? Are you offended because I said that?" Her expression changed quickly to one of guarded passivity.

"No, it's just that, it seemed like . . . . Oh never mind." We started walking again, then stopped at the street corner to wait for cars to pass. When the traffic was clear, we continued up the street.

"If you want to know how I cook, I told you. I have a pick-up truck with a camper. It has a bed and a stove in it. I even have a little television. Why is it that when elderly people do this, they call it retirement? But when I do it, it's called drifting."

"Because when they do it they've already lived their life, and now it's over, and, and . . . that doesn't make any sense to me either. Don't look at me that way! I'm perfectly aware that what I just said was ridiculous."

She looked at me with an enigmatic smile. I had no idea what she was thinking at the time, but I would've emptied my bank account to find out what it was. I opened the door to the ice cream shop and walked in. My blue-jean clad companion followed me inside, still smiling that maddening smile of hers.

Chapter Two

Once inside the ice cream shop, we slipped into a momentary silence while we pondered the vast array of choices before us. I decided on a vanilla low-fat frozen yogurt. My companion asked for a Rocky Road ice cream cone, double scoop. I paid the teenage boy at the counter, then started to sit down on the benches outside the store. She motioned for me to follow her, so I did.

"There's a better place to sit just up the road a bit. It's a little more private. That way we can talk without worrying about being overheard."

A sudden sense of panic hit me. I wasn't sure what place she was referring to, and I wasn't sure if I wanted to go to anywhere private with this self-proclaimed, rootless lesbian. She'd already made a couple of unnerving references to sexual intimacy. I wasn't sure what I was getting myself into. I was visibly relieved when she stopped at some public picnic tables just down the road from the ice cream shop.

She looked at me with a smirk on her face. "What's the matter? Did you think I was going to take you down some dark alley and smear Rocky Road all over you then lick it off?"

Angered by her words, I responded curtly, "Do you always make this many sexual remarks to strangers?"

"Why? How many have I made?"

"Three, in just twenty minutes."

"You're counting and timing me?" She shook her head as though I were a naughty little girl. "You're not earning many non-heterosexist points, I'm afraid. And yeah, I probably do make this many sexual innuendoes to strangers. When you move around a lot, most people you encounter in your life are strangers. Why waste time mincing words? I say what I think. I apologize if I've offended your yuppie senses, but that's just how I am. Perhaps you should think twice before you pick up vagrants on the beach."

"I didn't know you were a vagrant when I picked you up."

She laughed and shook her head, then looked at me sideways. "So you admit to picking me up?"

"What? Oh, I didn't realize that was what you meant."

"That's four." She held up four fingers and wriggled them at me.

"Please stop. You're making me uncomfortable, and I think you're doing it on purpose."

She smiled at me. "I am. Just wanted to show you how heterosexist you really are."

"What is it you want from me?"

"What do I want from you? I was the one who was sitting there on a log harmlessly playing my guitar when you came along and started staring at me. That usually precedes a pick-up line, which is usually followed by a night in the sack. What was I supposed to think? I'm the one who should be asking what it is you want from me. Or are you not in touch with yourself enough to realize you want?"

"Are you implying that I want to have sex with you?"

"Not necessarily. Are you inferring that I want to have sex with you?"

"No. Yes. I don't know. You're confusing me."

She laughed behind her ice cream cone. "Sorry," she said, though she looked completely impenitent.

"What's your name, anyway?"

"Why? Do you need to know that before we have sex? Do you want my history of lovers? My medical records?"

I started to get and up leave. She caught my arm and gently stopped me.

"I'm sorry. You're just so funny. You're trying so

hard not to appear heterosexist, and yet every time I make a sexually loaded comment, you get more uptight. Relax. I wasn't planning on taking you to bed with me tonight. That can wait. And I'm clean. I've been practicing safe sex since before the AIDS epidemic. There's more than one sexually transmitted disease going around."

I sat down again. "Look this isn't about sex. I just wanted to listen to your music."

The muscles in her face tightened for a moment, then relaxed again. When she spoke, her voice was suddenly soft and husky. "Yeah, well when you listen to my music, you're listening to my soul. That makes me feel pretty naked. Your sneaking up on me like that was kind of like me watching you undress in the window."

I covered my mouth with my hand, shocked by the realization that I had been very rude to this woman. I lowered my hand, then reached it out towards her. "I'm sorry. I didn't realize. That was insensitive of me to interrupt your reverie with my eavesdropping. I just felt compelled."

"Do you always follow through on your compulsions, or just the ones that aren't sexual?"

"Why is everything sexual to you? I just wanted to listen to your music. That's all. Apparently I shouldn't have done that. I said I was sorry. I'll stop pestering you."

I got up to leave again. I threw my empty yogurt cup into the trashcan, then started walking back to my house. She finished off her cone with a final slurp, then wiped her mouth on the napkin in her hand. When she had disposed of her garbage, she took several quick steps towards me to catch up. She stopped in front of me on the sidewalk, making it impossible for me to continue walking without detouring into the road. She put her hands on my upper arms and made me look into her eyes. Her smile had been replaced by a penetrating look of honesty.

"I don't think everything is sexual. I think everything is spiritual, including sex. My sexual side is part of my spiritual side, and it's also very much part of my musical side. You invaded my space in a moment of spiritual and emotional intimacy. I didn't think it would be polite if I just told you off, so I guess I've been needling you instead. I will stop. We came here to talk about you. So far we've talked mostly about me. Now it's your turn. And don't tell me your name, or you won't be telling your life story to a perfect stranger. That's why you don't need to know mine. It removes the anonymity. Isn't that what you wanted, a stranger to talk to?"

"I don't know what I want. You've got me completely confused."

"Honey, I think you were confused long before you met me. I'm just making you realize how confused you are."

"Why are you doing that?"

"I'm not doing it on purpose. Honestly. I had a lover once who told me I was a painful friend to have. She said that I was like a mirror. In order to be around me, you have to be willing to look at yourself in the mirror. To look truth in the eyes and deal with it. I guess it's my gift to the people around me. Trust me, I would give the gift to someone else if I could. It has made for more than one uncomfortable moment in my life. But it isn't something I can just stop doing. Or if I did, I wouldn't feel as though I were being honest."

I pushed past her and began walking up the street again. "God help me if I ever ran into you on a bad hair day!"

She caught up with me and fell into stride. "This has nothing to do with social niceties. I might tell you your hair looked horrible, or I might just ignore it, assuming you already know that, and don't need me to tell you. On the other hand, I would tell you if you had spinach in your teeth." She smiled a disarming smile.

"Good! But I hope you would do it gently. My husband points out all my faults, with glee almost. I think he likes exposing my flaws. He says he's just trying to help me, so I don't embarrass myself in public. But it feels like something more than that."

"Sounds like a real sweetheart."

"No, he's actually a nice guy."

"I see."

"There you go again. Writing me off. What does that 'I see' mean?"

"Nothing. It's just a reminder to myself that you can put your husband down, but I can't."

"I didn't mean it that way. I just didn't want you to get the wrong impression of Paul."

"Excuse me, but I don't giving a flying fig about Paul."

"No, I guess you wouldn't."

"I'll probably never even meet him, so it doesn't matter what I think of him."

"No, I suppose not."

"Can we change the subject, or is this what you need to talk about, your husband and his nit-picking?"

"I should let you go. I'm obviously wasting your time."

"Only if you think so."

"I don't know what I think."

"Now we're getting to it. You're really confused about something. What is it? Is this mid-life crisis time? If so, I'm the woman to talk to. I know all about those."

"Do you? How is that?"

"Later. You first."

"I don't know where to start. I didn't know I had anything to talk about until you asked if I needed someone to talk to. Suddenly I felt as though I desperately needed someone to talk to about my life. I realized that I have a whole bundle of emotions that have been wreaking havoc on my personal life, without my awareness. But where do I start?"

"How about with your sex life?"

"Oh please, let's not start that again."

She put up her hands in front of her, as though to ward off a blow from me. "No, no. I'm serious. How you feel about your sexual life is a good indicator as to how you feel about the rest of your life."

"Thank you, Dr. Ruth."

"I'm serious. How are you and your husband doing sexually?"

"Well, we usually have sex every Sunday morning. It's the only day of the week he sleeps in."

"How do you feel about that?" She stopped momentarily and shifted the weight of her guitar onto the opposite shoulder then proceeded.

I started to say something until I realized how close I was getting to my cottage. I took my companion by the elbow and steered her back down towards the beach. Then I said, "Would you like to take your guitar somewhere and set it down? I can't imagine that it would be very comfortable to carry it around on your back all the time."

"It's not that heavy, but my truck is down there, if you don't mind if I drop it off real quick."

I hesitated.

"Don't worry. I'm not planning on raping you in my camper. You can stay here if you'd like. I'll only be a few minutes."

Determined not to earn any more heterosexist points, I said, "No, it's okay, I'll walk with you."

"You have successfully changed the subject, but I'm going to ask the same question over and over again, until you get honest with yourself at least. Even if you don't tell me the truth. Tell yourself the truth. How do you feel about your sex life?"

I sighed. "It's boring."

"Have you told him that?"

"Are you kidding?"

"No, I'm not kidding. Tell him how you feel, then see what he does about it. That's a good way to test the waters."

I stopped and frowned at her. "What if I don't like what gets stirred up?"

She shook her head dismissively. "Then live with the boredom, I guess, or move on."

"Is that your answer to everything? Moving on?"

"Just about."

We arrived at the parking lot where her camper was

sitting. It was not what I had expected somehow. It was a nearly new green Ford pickup with shiny chrome wheels. The camper on the back was in mint condition as well. Aside from the light film of sea salt that attaches itself to everything on the coast, it seemed to be clean on the outside. When she opened the door, I discovered that the inside was more immaculate than either of my houses.

It was a small camper, but an efficient one. There was a full size bed in the loft over the cab of the truck. There were two swivel chairs, upholstered in brown velour, in what would be considered the living room. With a flick of her wrist, the room was transformed into a dining area. She had pulled a hidden table out of a panel on the wall, and locked it into place between the two chairs. The kitchenette was done in rich honey stained wood tones. There was a sink, a stove, and a refrigerator, all in miniature. There was also a toaster oven on the counter. On top of the kitchen cabinets was a bookshelf that contained several dozen books.

"Is there a bathroom in this place?"

"Yes, but it's very tiny. It matches the kitchen appliances. Do you need to use it? It's back there behind the cabinet. I usually use it only in the middle of the night when I don't have the wherewithal to put on clothes to go to the campground bathrooms."

"No, I was just curious. So where are you camping right now?"

"I found a place just north of town. It's quiet and fairly inexpensive."

"How long do you plan to stay there?"

"Now that all depends on what transpires in the next few days." She looked at me out of the corner of her eyes.

I looked at her coyly. "That's another innuendo, isn't it?"

She nodded, her eyes filled with merriment.

"I didn't get upset that time."

"No, you didn't. You get lots of non-heterosexist points for that."

"It's about time!"

She laughed, then visibly began warming up to her role as hostess.

"So can I get you something to drink? There's a Henry Weinhard's root beer in the fridge, and some orange juice, I think."

"I'll split the root beer with you."

"One root beer coming right up."

She opened one of the kitchen cabinets and pulled out two plastic cups. "I'll even use my best frosted mugs for you."

I smiled at her jest. "I guess it could get expensive to have glasses knocking around in the cupboards."

"Well, there's a way to do it, but I figure it's easier this way."

She twisted the cap off the bottle, and poured out the contents into the two cups. She handed me a cup, then lifted her own by way of a toast, "Here's to Henry, may he always give good head."

I shook my head at her, then lifted my cup. "To Henry. May he stay true to his roots."

She nearly choked on her drink. "That was good."

I beamed under her praise. "Why, thanks!"

She motioned for me to sit in one of the chairs, so I did. She took the other one, then leaned towards me. "So what do you think of my little home?"

"It's marvelous. I really like it. Very tiny, but efficient."

"Perfect for traveling light."

"Yes, I can see that. Like a turtle carrying its house on its back."

There was a moment of silence. Then the woman beside me picked up the guitar she had laid on her bed. She started strumming it, running her left hand up and down the neck, playing a tune I wasn't familiar with. When she was finished, I asked her, "What song was that?"

"One I'm in the process of writing. It doesn't have a name yet."

"It's kind of like you then."

"Have you decided you'd like to know my name

now?"

"No, I haven't, but mine's Rita." I thrust my hand towards her in a friendly gesture. She took it in her own, and pressed it firmly, but gently.

"Is that 'Rita' as in The Beatles' song?" She sang a line from the song, pronouncing the word meter with the same inflection they had used to make it rhyme with Rita.

"Yes, I got called that a lot when I was growing up."

"Somehow I'm not surprised."

"Did you write the song I listened to you playing on the beach?"

"Yes, I write all the songs I play."

"Would you play some for me, or is that still too intimate?"

"Well, it helps if I know when someone is listening. I didn't realize you were there until I was almost finished. I think my eyes had been closed."

"Yes, they were, for part of it. That helped to make the song more mesmerizing. I could tell you were really feeling what you were singing."

She smiled, almost shyly. "That's the intimate part."

I nodded in understanding. Then she began to play again. This time she beat out a hard rhythm on the strings, her foot tapping in time to the beat.

I'm running out of breath; and my pen's running out of ink
I don't know where to go, I cannot even think.
I've been searching for something, but I don't know what.
I act as though I'm free, and yet I know I'm caught.

Caught in a nightmare, and I can't wake up.
I'm locked in a room that is gonna blow up.
Running from myself, I'm running from this dream.
Running from the city with its glitter and gleam.

If there is an answer then it better come quickly

I need an overdose of reality.
I thought that getting high would surely set me free.
But now the walls are moving, darkness is closing in on me.

And I'm caught in a nightmare, and I can't wake up.
I'm locked in a room that is gonna blow up.
Running from myself, I'm running from this dream.
Running from the city with its glitter and gleam.

She repeated the chorus, then finished the song with a riveting rhythmic performance. She looked over at me, something she hadn't done throughout the entire song. She had either stared at the floor or kept her eyes closed. She looked as though she expected me to say something.

"Wow! That was something."

"You didn't like it."

"No, I did like it. It was very powerful. It was like you were singing your heart out. That must take an awful lot of energy."

"That's not all it takes, Rita."

"What do you mean?"

"It takes a lot of trust for me to pour out my soul in a song like that. That's the very core part of me that's singing."

"Thank you for trusting me enough to play for me. You don't have to keep on, if you don't want to."

"No, I like singing for you. I can tell you feel what I'm saying. I'm not just a radio blaring in the background to you."

"I do feel what you're saying. Your songs make me want to ask you all kinds of questions about yourself.'

"Like what?'

"What are you running from? Is that why you don't stay in one place? And do you still do drugs?"

"I don't know that I am running from anything. I wrote that song when I was in college, as a memorial to having buried my drug habit five years previous to that time. I quit doing drugs just before my junior year in high school."

"What did you study in college?"

She smiled slightly, as though embarrassed. "You'll laugh."

"I won't laugh."

"The Bible."

I snickered. I couldn't help it. It caused such cognitive dissonance to be sitting here talking to this woman who was a songwriting, guitar-playing, lesbian vagabond. Just minutes before she had me seriously convinced that she was about to abscond with my person. It was amusing to find that she had studied the Bible in college.

"I told you you'd laugh."

"I'm sorry, but you were right. That is rather hilarious. How did that happen?"

"Well, I had gotten pretty heavily into the drug scene in the seventies. I was searching for truth, not just an escape from life's pressure. I wanted answers. I thought I might be able to find them in drugs. When I didn't, I turned to Christianity. When I didn't find them there either, I began to look inside myself."

"Did you find your answers there?"

"Sort of. I'm still finding them. That's what this camper is all about, and the wandering. I'm just living for the moment in a society that tells us we should live for the future, while remaining mired in the past."

"So does that mean you're into Zen?"

"No, not really. I'm not into anything formally. I find philosophical and spiritual teachings of all kinds interesting and helpful. But mostly I try to find the truth within. So far I'm to the point where I realize that life is the journey. It's not the end of the road I need to be concerned about, but the road itself. So I took to the road literally, in order to reinforce that truth, I guess."

"Hm. That's rather interesting."

"Is it?"

"Yes, it is. So, Pilgrim, what is your name?"

"Tired of the anonymity or just curious?"

"Both."

"It's Beth."

"Beth. Hmm, that fits."

She cocked her head to one side. "Does it now?"

I nodded my head. "Yes, it does."

She set her guitar down. "Good. I'm glad you approve. I'd hate to think I'd lived all these years with the wrong name." Her eyes sparkled at me.

A little uncomfortable with the silence that followed, I said abruptly, "Is there a pay phone nearby?"

Beth looked startled. "I haven't a clue. Why?"

"I need to call me husband to tell him I'm all right. I don't want him to worry. It's starting to get dark out there. I've been gone for over an hour."

She pulled a cellular telephone out of a backpack that sat on the floor behind her chair, and offered it to me. "Here. Knock yourself out."

I took it from her. "Thanks. This place really has all the comforts of home, doesn't it?"

She smiled. "Most of them."

I called my house, and left a message on the answering machine. I wondered where Paul was, more out of curiosity than caring. I figured he must've gone to town to pick up something to eat or drink. We hadn't yet fully stocked the house for our week's vacation. Mostly because I hadn't been in the mood to plan anything.

I told the answering machine to tell Paul that I would be home later. I had run into a friend, and was having a good time talking with her. I told him not to worry, even though I knew he'd get caught up in some television program, and not even notice I wasn't there. Then I hung up and handed the phone back to Beth.

"Not there, huh? I hope he isn't out looking for you."

I had to laugh at that one. "No, he wouldn't be out looking for me. We aren't that kind of couple. We don't keep a close an eye on each other. He goes his way; I go mine. Sometimes I wonder why we ever married."

"Have you ever come up with a good reason?'

"No, I haven't, I'm sorry to say. It was convenience mostly. I met Paul when I was in college. He asked me out, so we started dating. He asked me to marry him, and I consented. Then I quit school to help support him while he finished law school."

"Why didn't you wait until you'd gotten your degree before you married him?"

"At the time, I didn't really have a reason for going to college. I was doing it because my parents wanted me to become a teacher, so I'd have something to fall back on, if I couldn't find a good husband. But I found a good husband. They liked Paul, and thought he was an excellent choice, so I got a marriage certificate instead of a degree. College wasn't important to me anyway. In fact, I was relieved to be able to throw my books aside and get a job to help Paul."

"What did you do?"

"I worked for my father in the one of the department stores he owned. He put me in the housewares department, figuring it would be a good way for me to learn more about homemaking. He was right. I learned everything I needed to know about becoming a good lawyer's wife. I learned about decorating and entertaining. All those wonderful skills that make a man glad he picked you."

My tone was becoming more and more acidic the longer I talked. The bitterness I felt welling up inside me was a surprise. I continued talking. "Now I'm his liaison on the social ladder in the law firm. I plan the parties and the dinners, while he jockeys for position in the legal world. The better social wife I am, the better he looks to the firm."

"I see."

"Now there you go again. What have you concluded about me this time?"

"I think what I concluded in the beginning."

"Oh, so you were right in thinking I was a . . . how did you put it?"

"A yuppie heterosexist woman."

"Is that really what you think?"

"From where I'm sitting, you don't look as though you're happy with your life. Sometimes being a success in the eyes of the world requires a prostitution of the soul."

"Are you telling me I sold my soul to be successful?"

"No, I'd say you sold your soul for security."

I found myself getting angry, more at myself than at Beth. But it was easier to blame her for my discomfort than it was to take responsibility for my own choices. "And just what was I suppose to do? Become an elementary school teacher, and wipe snotty noses all day?"

"Look, I'm not trying to tell you what you should have done with your life, and I'm not saying that what you did was wrong. You did what you thought you should do. We all make decisions we regret later, even though they seemed like the best thing to do at the time. The important thing now is to find out what you want to do with your life from this moment on. Is there anything you love to do that you could turn into a career?"

"I'm not sure. Perhaps. I'll have to ponder that later. Right now, I think I could stand to use your bathroom."

Beth got up, and looked out the window of the camper. "I'll tell you what. I'll walk with you over to the public restroom in the park over there. Then we can both go, and you won't have to try to use that microscopic toilet in there. You have to be a contortionist just to pee. Better yet, I'll just pull the truck around there so we don't have to walk through the park at night. I don't know how safe it is out here after dark."

"Me neither. We don't get to spend much time at our cottage, even though I'd really like to. I like Cannon Beach. I wish we could live here instead of Portland."

"Why can't you?"

"Paul's career is centered there."

"He couldn't move it out here?"

"Not without a great deal of trouble. Besides Paul loves Portland."

"Does Rita love Portland?"

I picked at a loose thread on my blouse. "Not really.

I mean, it's all right, I suppose, but I prefer the beach to the city."

Beth nodded, then opened the camper door. "Just sit tight. I'll drive the truck around." She walked around to the cab of the pickup, and drove us over to the restrooms. I sat in silence wondering what it would be like to live in Cannon Beach year around.

Chapter Three

After our bathroom break, we settled ourselves into the camper again. Beth started rummaging around in the cabinets. "Are you hungry?"

"A little. What time is it anyway?" I looked for the wristwatch that was conspicuously absent from my wrist. "I should probably go home."

"It's nine o'clock. Do you want to call Paul again to see if he's back yet?"

The thought of going home to Paul was decidedly disagreeable, so I hoped Beth wasn't anxious to be alone again. "No. He's all right. So what are you finding to eat in there?"

She displayed her discoveries for me. "Corn chips or cheddar cheese popcorn. Which will it be?"

A surge of excitement rushed through me, and I felt as though I were on my way to a teenage slumber party. "How about the popcorn? And some water too, if you don't mind."

"Don't mind a bit," Beth replied cheerfully. "Hand me your cup so I can rinse it out." She got out a bowl and dumped in the popcorn, then poured us both a cup of cold water. She sat down across the table from me, and began to toss popcorn into her mouth.

"How do you keep the refrigerator cold while you're parked out here?"

"I use a variety of methods. Mostly I run the fridge off a separate battery that I recharge either with regular electric current, or through the solar panels on the roof, whichever is most readily available at the moment."

"You're pretty self-sufficient then."

"I try to be, in more ways than one."

"I'm beginning to see that," I said thoughtfully. "I guess you think I've sold myself short, huh?"

"That's not for me to say."

I put my hand over the one she had resting on the table, and felt the warmth of it enter my body. I tried not to notice how safe it made me feel. "Now be honest with me. I'd like to know how my life looks from someone else's perspective."

She moved her hand nonchalantly away from mine, and retrieved a piece of popcorn that had leaped onto the floor of the camper. "I don't know you very well, obviously, but I would say that your life is beginning to seem a little empty to you. You did what your parents wanted you to, had brought you up to do, and now you're bored. It may be nothing more than a mid-life crisis. You may go through some serious soul-searching, only to find that it's not so bad after all."

"You really think so?"

"No."

"Then why did you say that?"

"Because I thought you might need some reassurance that your whole world wasn't crumbling to dust."

A wave of self-pity washed over me, causing tears to well up in my eyes. "It is crumbling, isn't it? I don't know why I didn't see it until now. I've had nagging doubts before about my marriage, but I dismissed them as silly."

"And you may dismiss them again as silly. Who knows how you'll feel tomorrow when you wake up?" She squeezed my forearm reassuringly.

"What do you think I should do?"

"How am I supposed to know?"

"I don't know. You seem to have it all together. You don't need society's approbation. You're content to do exactly what you want to do, when you want to do it. You're free, Beth. Truly free. Isn't that an exhilarating feeling?"

"Not always. It was at first."

"When did you become a drifter?"

"I think I've always been a drifter inside. I just didn't know how to live the reality of it. I've been driving this camper for close to five years now. All over America and Canada. One of these days, I want to backpack across Europe. I almost bought myself a Eurail pass last year. I did get my passport, just in case."

"What did you do before you started traveling?"

"Oh, I went from job to job, just trying to find something that would hold my interest for more than a year or two. I never found anything that did. Except music."

"Why don't you pursue that? Make records and do concerts."

"Too lazy, I suppose. It's not as though I have a great deal of mass appeal. A lot of my songs have a very lesbian point of view. There aren't that many lesbian bars and bookstores in this country. I've been to most of them, so I should know. I suppose I could sell my records myself, if it came to that, but I'm just not sure that's what I want to do."

"You're really good though. I think you could be successful at it."

"I'm not sure I want to be successful. There's a price to pay for being Melissa Etheridge or k.d. lang. I'm not sure I'm willing to pay that price. I like being able to sit and play my guitar in public, without being surrounding by hordes of fans. Besides when you're famous, you never know whether people love you for yourself, or for your fame, or even for your talent. I don't want to have to wonder about that."

"So you hide behind obscurity?"

"Perhaps. I don't know. What do you think? How does my life look from where you're sitting?" She looked at me as though she were only mildly curious about what I thought of her life. I got the feeling that my opinion wouldn't mean a whole lot to her, and that she was merely engaging in polite conversation.

"Well, part of me thinks that it would be romantic just to drive off, and leave all my responsibilities behind."

"Now hold on there. I have responsibilities too. I have to make sure I stay solvent. I have to keep the truck in tiptop condition. I have to keep up with the maintenance on the camper, inside and out. I have plenty of responsibilities. They're just different from the ones I had before. They're ones I feel I can live with happily, which is more than I can say about my former responsibilities."

"All right, so you have responsibilities too. I guess what I was saying is that it would be nice to get away from my particular set of responsibilities. Which reminds me. Could I borrow your phone again? I think I will try to get Paul again. I hadn't planned to be gone this long."

She handed me the phone. Then she leaned back in her chair, put her hands behind her head, and closed her eyes. Again there was no answer at the cottage, so I left another message explaining that we were having so much fun talking that I might not be home for awhile.

Beth sat up again, and looked at me as though she were really interested in what I had to say. "Do you think I'm running from something?"

"What makes you think that this silly woman has an answer for that?"

"Just looking for pearls of wisdom, I suppose. It's an old habit."

"I think it's great that you're living out what you believe to be true about the world. I think that's a courageous thing to do. I don't think I could do it, no matter how dissatisfied I may be with my life."

She nodded. "So it's back to your old life tomorrow?"

"What else can I do?"

"I can think of lots of things."

"Like what?"

"Like figure out what you would do if you had all the money you needed to do it. Would you leave Paul?

Would you go back to college? Would you sell everything, and buy a camper and a pick-up, and travel all around the world?"

"I might travel, though not in a camper. Not if I had all the money I needed to do what I wanted."

She leaned forward in her chair, "What then? What would you do, Rita?"

I shifted in my chair, leaning back away from the intense energy she radiated. "Let me see. Yes, I think I would leave Paul. Then I might travel around the world."

"What places would you visit?"

"Rome, Paris, Athens, the Swiss Alps, London. That's all I can name at the moment, though I'm sure I could think of more, if I gave myself the chance."

"Okay, so Europe and the Mediterranean. Good start. What else would you do?"

"I would buy my parents a yacht. They've always wanted one, or at least my father has."

"That's great, but we're talking about you right now. What would you do for Rita? New clothes?"

"Yes, but not anything like what I own now. I have a wardrobe big enough to clothe an army of women. It's part of the image, you know, not wearing the same outfit twice. I do it anyway, but I try to be careful as to when and where."

"What else?"

"I think I'd . . ."

"Yes?"

"I think I'd buy a house at Cannon Beach, and live here year around."

She finally leaned back in her chair, releasing me from her probing stare. "It is a nice place, isn't it?"

"Yes, it is. Are you thinking about staying here?"

She smiled slightly. "There's that question again."

"I'm sorry. I keep trying to pin you down. I'm just curious about your life. I can't imagine anyone not liking Cannon Beach enough to want to stay here forever."

"I'm not sure I could stand the weather for long periods of time."

"You'd get used to it."

"Yeah, and then I'd get bored with it."

"I don't think I would ever get bored with it. It seems to match my mood."

"But my moods change."

"So do mine, and fortunately so does the weather. I know there's a lot of fog and drizzle, but I still think I'd like to live here year around."

She leaned up again, and placed a hand on my knee, completely unnerving me. "Then do it!"

Startled by the pressure of her hand on my leg, I forgot what we were talking about. "What?"

"Just do it! If it's what you want, go for it. If you want to travel, then travel. If you want to live in Cannon Beach, then move here. You already have a house here." She sat back in her chair and folded her arms across her chest.

Missing the warmth of her hand on my knee, I said quietly, "It's not that simple."

"I never said it was simple. Do you think it was simple for me to sell my house and most of my possessions? Do you think it was simple to pick out just the right truck and camper set-up? Do you think it was simple to tell all my family and friends 'Hey, listen up, I'm going to live in a camper now? Here's how you can get in contact with me.' Believe me, it wasn't simple."

"I suppose not. But I'll have to think about it."

"I highly recommend that. Just don't lose your nerve. It will be much harder once you go back to Portland with Paul."

I mulled over the idea of going anywhere with Paul. I realized that somewhere deep inside of me was a person who was longing desperately to escape from her prison. I wondered if she would make it.

She leaned forward again, and I wondered if she would put her hand back on my leg. Much to my disappointment, all she said was, "Shall I drive you back to your place?"

"What? Oh, yes. That would be kind of you."

Her eyes were smiling when she looked at me. "Got you thinking, didn't I? Well, that's good. You just sleep on all that." She patted my knee lightly, then stood up. "You want to ride in the cab with me, or sit back here in the comfort zone?"

"I'll ride up front with you. I'd like to see the world through your window."

"Well, in that case, why don't we take a ride first?"

"Where to?"

"I don't know. Let's just drive, shall we?"

So we did just that. We headed south on 101, and drove along the coast. We talked and talked as the miles sped by. As we conversed, I found that slowly but surely, Beth was peeling back the layers of my self-defensiveness, and knocking down the walls of assumption and projection. I learned a lot about myself that night.

Somewhere between Tillamook and Lincoln City, we found a coffee shop, and propped our eyelids open with a couple cups of java. We decided then to head back before we were no longer able to find our way, for lack of sleep. We finally made it back to Cannon Beach around two in the morning. By that time, we were feeling pretty silly. Beth drove me home, then waited patiently while I searched my pockets for the keys to the cottage. When I realized I didn't have them with me, I looked at her and burst out laughing.

"I can't get in without waking Paul. I didn't bring the keys with me. I was just going to take a walk on the beach, and then go to town for a few groceries."

"Can you ring the doorbell?"

"There is no doorbell, and our bedroom is on the ocean side of the house. That side is on stilts because of the slope back there. I could throw rocks at the window, but Paul is a very sound sleeper. I doubt if he'd hear me."

"What do you want to do then? Can we break in through a window?"

"Not without breaking the windows themselves. Unless Paul opened a window after I left, they are all shut and locked. He hates fresh air, for some reason, so if he opened a window, it would be a first. I've spent fifteen years opening windows, and he has spent it going around behind me closing them again."

"Well, I guess we can sit up and talk all night. I don't have to be anywhere tomorrow, and neither do you, I hope."

"Hey, I'm on vacation. The only plans I had for tomorrow were for sleeping late, walking on the beach, and maybe figuring out what we were going to do for meals the rest of the week."

"Do you want to leave Paul a note on the front door, so he won't worry?"

"That's a thought. I can slip something in the mail slot. That way he'll find it, if he wakes up. Though I sincerely doubt he will wake up. If he hasn't missed me yet, he's not likely to miss me now." I pulled a pen out of my jacket pocket, and started trying to scratch out a few words on the back of an old bank deposit slip.

"Shouldn't we try to knock, just in case he's up and is worried about you?"

"Paul worried about me? Don't be silly. If he listened to the answering machine, he will know what I'm up to, if not where I am exactly. Do you have anything to write with? This pen doesn't seem to want to work."

She reached over and opened the glove compartment, then handed me a ballpoint pen. "Here, I think this one works."

I scribbled a note explaining my dilemma, then got out of the truck and walked up to the front of the house. I tried to look in the windows, but couldn't see anything because all the lights were turned off, except for the porch light. I slipped the note in the mail slot on the door, then went back to the truck.

"No sign of life within. He must've gone to bed long ago."

"Where to now?"

"I don't know. I'm pretty tired."

"Me too. I don't think I can drive any more tonight. We might end up in a ditch."

"Can we go to your campground?"

"Sure. If you want, I can sleep in the chairs back there, and you can sleep in the bed."

"Don't be silly. You sleep in the bed. I'll sleep in the chairs."

"Well, we can fight about that after we get there. Hop in, and fasten your seatbelt, Rita. We're going for another ride."

We drove to the campground, just north of downtown Cannon Beach. As we pulled in, our headlights shone on a couple raccoons that were playing in the trees above the campsite next to Beth's. In the dark of night, the lush green trees of the campground made the area look like an enchanted forest.

"Now don't go messing around with the raccoons when you get out. They look cute, but they can get pretty feisty. Sometimes they carry rabies. And if you ever start feeding them, they won't leave you alone.   Just hurry around to the door of the camper, and I'll be right behind you."

I did as she suggested. She came up behind me and unlocked the door. She opened it, and gestured for me to go first. I wondered whether she might be watching my backside as I stepped in ahead of her.   For some inexplicable reason, I found myself hoping she was. Once inside, she shut and locked the door behind us. She told me to sit down while she got things ready. The camper was too small for both of us to be moving around at the same time. She opened a drawer and pulled out an unopened toothbrush.

"Here, I was about to switch toothbrushes, but I'll let you have it instead."

"You don't have to do that."

"It's just a toothbrush, Rita, and I assume you don't happen to be carrying one on you."

"No, I don't generally carry one everywhere I go. Thanks."

I watched as she pulled back the covers on the bed. Then she picked up one of the pillows, and was bringing down with her. Much to my surprise, I found myself saying, "Look, we're both adult women here. I don't mind sharing a bed, if you don't.'

She stopped what she was doing to look at me. "Okay. If that's what you want."

"But you have to grant me several more non-heterosexist points for that."

She smiled a smile so radiant, it would've made the sun jealous had it been around to see it. "You got it. I'll even sleep next to the wall. That way you can escape easier should my dreams cause me to become passionate in my sleep." She grinned slyly at me.

"You're teasing me."

"You're getting better at figuring that out."

"I think your bark is worse than your bite."

"I wouldn't say that exactly, but let's just say I don't force myself on women. That's definitely not my style."

"Then I'm safe."

"For now, at least." She winked at me, and crawled up into the loft.

Inside I was somewhat disappointed that she had assured me so readily that she would be honorable. I found myself getting more and more curious about what it would be like to be with a woman like Beth. She was intriguing, to say the least.

Chapter Four

After we positioned ourselves carefully in the bed, I found myself more awake than I imagined I could be at that time of the night. I was not in the habit of keeping late hours, so it surprised me to discover that I couldn't keep my eyes closed to save my life. I looked over at Beth, and as my eyes adjusted to the darkness, discerned that she was looking at me. I was suddenly in a talkative mood, so I starting talking again.

"Are you awake?"

"Yeah. I don't usually fall asleep the second my

head hits the pillow."

"I suppose that was a pretty stupid question."

"Though at this time of the night, anything is possible."

"You're not usually a late nighter?"

"No, I've found there's very little to do late at night except read. In campgrounds most people get up with the sun, so it's not wise to stay up too late, unless you're a really sound sleeper."

"Do you ever meet interesting people in campgrounds?"

"Oh yeah. Just yesterday I was talking to a couple from England. They told me all about the camping trip they were doing. They flew into San Francisco, and are camping their way up the coast to Seattle."

"Really? How exciting. Now when you say 'couple,' do you mean a married couple or a lesbian couple?"

"Neither. I just meant a couple of humans. It was a man and a woman, but I have no idea whether they were married. I don't usually check for rings, or ask personal questions like that."

"No, I suppose not. So where do you meet women lovers?"

"That depends. If I'm in a town with a lesbian bar or gay bookstore, then I hang around there trying to meet people. I often arrange impromptu concerts. I do them for free, then take donations. Most places let me perform if they have a moment for me to audition. Some just take a chance on me without the audition. They don't have anything to lose usually. After I play for awhile, I have no trouble finding women who want to talk to me. Being in the spotlight makes it very easy to meet people."

"I've never been to a lesbian bar. Is there one here?"

"If there is, I haven't found it yet. I haven't explored the town much though, except to notice that there's a theater here, and some interesting art galleries. I've been hanging out on the beach mostly."

"Did you buy your Birkenstocks at the store in

town?"

"I did. My old ones were pretty beaten up. I'm going to have to see about getting them resoled. There's a place in the Seattle area that does a good job repairing them."

"You've been to Seattle?"

"Of course. What traveling lesbian would miss out on an opportunity to visit all the lesbian Meccas?"

"Seattle is a lesbian Mecca?"

"You better believe it."

"I didn't know that. I used to live there."

"Didn't you noticed an awful lot of gay people when you were there?"

"Well, of course, but they're pretty prevalent in Portland too."

"There is that. I forgot you lived in Portland."

I found myself suddenly interested in all the little details of lesbian life. "So what do lesbians do for fun?"

I sensed rather than saw the scowl on her face. "Now wait a minute. What's that supposed to mean? Are we talking sexual fun or fun fun?"

"Just plain old fun."

"Well, I can't speak for the entire galactic empire, but I would say pretty much what other people do for fun. We go to the beach and the theater. We rent videos and eat popcorn. We walk hand in hand in the moonlight when we feel safe."

"When you feel safe?"

"Yeah, you know, as in, I wouldn't dare try walking down the streets of Birmingham holding my girlfriend's hand, but Seattle would be all right."

"I don't think I understand."

"Gay bashing, Rita. People like to beat up gay people in some parts of this country. In some parts of the world, they execute them. Legally. You don't pay much attention to politics, do you?"

"Only if it affects my husband's career."

"I take it he doesn't care about gays and lesbians, and the civil rights issues we're fighting for."

"I have no idea what he cares about besides winning his cases."

"Sounds like a deep man."

I started to defend him, then thought to myself, "Why bother?" I propped myself up on one arm, and looked in Beth's direction. She had backed into the corner of the bed, so I couldn't tell whether she still had her eyes open. I ventured to ask another question, hoping she hadn't fallen asleep in the interim. "What do you care about, Beth?"

"Far too many things to enumerate at this hour of the night."

"I see."

"Do you see, Rita?"

I could feel the laughter in her voice warming my heart. I knew it was getting ridiculously late, but I just couldn't bring myself to end our conversation. "No, it's too dark to see much of anything at the moment, but perhaps you'll give me a rain check on the answer some time."

"Fair enough. Your wish is granted."

"Wow. I didn't know it was so easy to have a wish granted. Could you grant me another wish?"

"That all depends on the wish. There are limits to my powers. I'm not actually a fairy after all, just a dyke, and a sleepy one at that. But fire away. I'll do what I can."

"Would you kiss me?"

There was a long pause. A very long pause. I wondered for a minute if she had fallen asleep, yet I knew that question was too loaded for that to happen. The initially soothing sounds of the night grew into a cacophony in my ears, as I awaited her answer.

Finally she exhaled very loudly and slowly. "No, I won't do that. I don't kiss heterosexual women who are merely curious as to what it would be like to kiss a lesbian. And I don't kiss women who are involved with other people."

After that lengthy silence, I wasn't too shocked by her answer, but I didn't want to leave it there. I wanted her to know what she was doing to me. I waited a few seconds while the tension built up again. "Do you kiss women who are falling in love with you?"

She laughed quietly into her pillow. Although I couldn't see it, I just knew there was a smirk on her face as she said, "Why? Do you see anyone around here who meets those requirements?"

I reached over and touched her shoulder. "Only me."

She took my hand off her shoulder, and held it for a moment, then released it back into my care. "Rita, you've done a lot of soul-searching tonight. I think we should leave it at that. Okay? It's late, and I can't say that I'm very awake. That kind of thing should wait until we both have our wits about us. I think I left mine somewhere around Tillamook, and it's too late to go looking for them now. Perhaps another time. I'm flattered by your request, but I think it best to deny your wish for now."

I moved over towards her. I could hear her breathing. I could feel the warmth radiating from her body.

"Rita, I don't think that's a good idea."

I scooted in closer. Close enough for me to see the shape of her face and the interest in her eyes. Then I pressed my lips against hers. It was a soft, gentle kiss. She returned it hesitantly at first. Then as I began to grow more passionate, she did too. When our lips parted company, she put her hand up to my cheek and brushed the hair away from my eyes. I grabbed her hand and laid it on my breast.

"No, Rita. Not tonight. I can't. I just can't. I would feel as though I were taking advantage of your emotional vulnerability right now. Sleep on that kiss tonight. Then tell me what you want in the morning. Okay?"

I held her hand against my body, not wanting to let it go. I was afraid I'd never have another chance like this in my life. I didn't want it to slip away. I began to maneuver her hand so she was kneading my breast. "Please, Beth. I may never have another chance to have this experience. I won't be sorry tomorrow. I promise. If I decide it's not what I want for my life, then I'll leave you alone."

She jerked her hand away from me. I could feel the hurt in her words, as she said, "That's just fine, Rita, but what about me? What happens to my heart if I make love to you tonight, only to find that it was just a phase for you. This isn't a phase for me. I live here in this body of mine. I live here in this heart you seem so willing to treat casually. What about me, Rita? You've got Paul. Who do I have to return home to, if you decide it was just a fluke? Just a result of too much coffee, and too little sleep. Where do I go to escape the memory of your betrayal? I don't have sex casually, and I don't treat love lightly."

Angered by her words, I said, "Now wait a minute. Aren't you the one who moves on after the relationship bottoms out? Doesn't that seem just a teensy bit hypocritical to you?"

"Sometimes it takes years for a relationship to bottom out. I've never had one bottom out overnight. I don't do one night stands. If that's what this is all about, then I don't want to have anything to do with it."

"So what you're saying is that if we had a relationship, you might hang around for years?"

"That's not what I said, but that is a possibility, as long as the relationship was healthy for both of us. As long as we were both being benefited by it."

"But what about your need to move on?"

"Rita, you're the one who called me a drifter. I agreed with it because I figured that was what you wanted to see. What makes you think that what I'm wandering all over the country looking for isn't a love that doesn't bottom out? I don't know if there is such a thing, but I'm certainly interested in finding it if it does exist."

"Beth, kiss me again. I want to be kissed by you willingly, passionately. That is, if you have come to feel anything for me. I know this is rather sudden, but I feel so hungry for a new life. I need change. I need to be jolted from the dreariness of my old life."

She huffed in disgust, then rolled over onto her back. "I see. You're bored with your yuppie lifestyle and your sex life, so you want to jazz it up with a quick and painless affair with a lesbian. No need to worry about getting pregnant. No need to worry about explaining your spending the night with a girlfriend. Is that it? Damn, it could even make your fantasies a little more exciting. Perhaps you could even talk Paul into joining in. Am I getting warm yet?"

She stopped talking when she realized I was crying. She turned towards me, and tried to wipe the tears from my cheeks. "I'm sorry. I've hurt you. I'm tired. I got carried away. Forgive me, Rita. I'm confused and scared."

Through my tears I said, "You're scared? What are you scared of? Me?"

"Yes, you. I've really enjoyed talking to you. If you weren't married, I would've kissed you already, I bet. But look at it from my perspective for a moment. How do I know you won't walk away tomorrow with my heart in your pocket? How do I know you won't walk off and have a good laugh with your husband about this?"

"Beth, I can't guarantee what tomorrow will bring. I will say this, however. I'm not playing with your emotions. I am attracted to you. I sense that you may be attracted to me too. I don't have any guarantees that you won't drive off into the sunset tomorrow. We're in the same boat."

"We are not! You're married. That's M-A-R-R-I-E-D. Married, with a capital "L" for legal. I have no one bound to me by law or by promise. I have no vows echoing in the corridors of my memories, no wedding pictures yellowing in the albums. No legal documents, signed and witnessed, and validated by the state. None of that. We are not in the same boat."

"You're right. I'm sorry. It is all very complicated. I guess I was being selfish. I wanted to look before I leaped into a lesbian relationship. I wanted to see if it felt right to me before I announced to the world that I wish to leave my husband, so I can live my life as a lesbian. But I'm going to leave my husband whether I sleep with you tonight, or any other night."

Clearly startled, Beth asked, "When did you decide

that?"

"I have no idea. Maybe just now. I can't believe I'm lying here begging you to touch me. What a difference. I know I wouldn't have to beg a man to have sex with me, wedding ring or not. I guess it's different with lesbians. Here, I'll even turn over my wedding rings to you. You can hang onto them until I return tomorrow."

I pulled off my wedding band and engagement ring, and attempted to give them to her. She gently pushed my hand away.

"Please keep your rings, Rita."

She breathed deeply and slowly, and appeared to be thinking hard about her reply. Finally she said, "Listen I can't speak for all lesbians. I'm only one person. It's true that even though I've only just met you, I have come to care for you. Through all our soul-bearing talks, I've come to see a little bit of who you are, and yes, I am interested and attracted to you. But I don't want to hold your rings as hostage, and I'm not going to take advantage of your vulnerability." She paused for a moment, then said in a softer tone, "It would mean more to me if you'd just let me hold you tonight."

When she pulled me over to her side of the bed I thought she might be giving in after all. I greatly underestimated her self-control. She put her arms around me, and held me the rest of the night. Not once did her hands stray. Not once did I feel her lips on any part of my body, other than those first kisses I shamelessly stole from her.

Chapter Five

When the first rays of sunlight began prying their way into the camper, I wriggled out from under the covers, and ventured outside in search of a bathroom. I found one quickly, much to the relief of my strained bladder. I took a moment to brush my teeth with the toothbrush Beth had given me. After I had finished, I shook the excess water out of the brush, then looked closely at it's violet translucence. I held the toothbrush to my chest as I thought of Beth. It was her first gift to me. Then I realized how ridiculously juvenile I was being, so I laid it on the sink, and ran my hands through my hair. I stared long and hard at the disheveled reflection in the mirror. I pined for a hairbrush, my curling iron, and some hair spray.

What a mess I looked. My hair was unkempt; my clothes were wrinkled from sleeping in them. My makeup had worn off. If she hadn't wanted me last night, then she certainly wasn't going to want me this morning. But there wasn't a darn thing I could do about my appearance, so I headed back to the camper. I entered quietly, not wishing to wake my sleeping companion. I climbed back into bed with her, and tried to go back to sleep. When that didn't work, I tried staring at her for awhile, mesmerized by her unblemished complexion. She didn't seem to use any makeup whatsoever, and yet her skin was flawless. Her indigo hair was revealing its bluish highlights in the morning sun, as it lay spread out on her pillow. I stared at her, then noticed her eyelids twitching. She opened her eyes just a little bit and looked at me. She gave me a sleepy smile that melted my heart.

"Hi there. You're certainly looking perky this morning," she whispered in a husky voice.

"Good morning, Beth. Did you sleep well?"

She nodded and opened her eyes a little more. Then she yawned. "I'll be awake in a minute. Then I can drive you home. I hope you haven't been waiting long for me to wake up. I'm not used to staying up so late."

"I'm in no hurry."

"No? I wondered if you had come to your senses."

"Which is supposed to mean what exactly? That I've realized that I haven't enough courage to decide how I'm going to spend the rest of my life?"

"That isn't how I would've put it."

"How would you put it?"

"Something along the lines of you've realized that

Paul isn't such a bad guy, and it was crazy to risk your marriage for a night in the sack with a nomadic lesbian."

"I see."

"Uh oh. I know that's not good. What did I say wrong?"

"Nothing. I just wish you would let me have my mid-life crisis without assuming that nothing is going to change. I hate to tell you this, but it has already changed. I've changed inside completely, metamorphosed in a single day. Hard to believe perhaps, but it's been a long time in coming. I can't go back to thinking the way I used to think, and I can't go back to living the way I used to live. Even if you choose to disappear without a trace, I'm going to leave Paul. It's not as though I had been mad at him, and now I'm over it. It's that I realized some time yesterday that I feel wretched inside living out this lie I have called 'my life' for the past fifteen years.

"I have nothing against Paul as a man. He's decent enough. He's a good husband, I suppose. I just don't want to continue pretending that we love each other when it's obvious that we don't, and probably never did. I think we will both be relieved when the charade is over."

"Don't be too sure of that."

"Okay, so I'll be relieved. He'll probably be annoyed because he won't have anyone to organize his personal life any more. But once he overcomes that minor irritation, he'll find a new wife, and go on his merry way. It's that simple. He will do some problem solving, blame me for the divorce, and then get remarried. I, on the other hand, will continue this gut-wrenching, soul-searching journey until I find . . . "

"Until you find what?"

"I don't know. Me, I suppose. That is what this is all about, isn't it? Finding myself. What does Rita want to do with her life? Where does Rita want to live? Who the hell is Rita? Aren't I being a typical, spoiled American? Those of us who can afford it, have a mid-life crisis, and forge a new path towards wholeness, leaving behind the shards of broken promises and shattered dreams."

"You worry me, Rita. You're starting to sound too much like me."

"Well, you're not the only one allowed the luxury of cynicism."

"I guess you put me in my place."

I hit her in the face with my pillow. She picked it up and put it between us.

"Is that supposed to be a boundary line I shouldn't step over?"

"I don't think so. I think it's just a pillow. Did you want me to hit you with it in retaliation?"

"That's what usually happens in pillow fights."

"In my experience what usually follows a pillow fight is tickling, and then sex. At least that's what usually happened in college when the initial sexual tension got too much to stand."

"Oh."

"Has that been your experience too?"

"No. I've never had a pillow fight before."

She rolled onto her side, propping herself up on one elbow. "You are kidding me, aren't you?"

I turned my body to face her squarely. "No, but I'd like to try it some time."

"The pillow fight, or what follows?"

"Both."

"I see."

"Finally!"

I picked up the pillow and hit her with it again. She tossed it on the floor, and pulled me into her arms.

"I'm a lover, Rita, not a fighter. Let's skip the pillow fight foreplay, shall we?"

She kissed me softly on the lips, her tongue exploring the rim of my mouth. She pulled back and looked at me, smiling. "Hey, it's not fair for one of us to have morning breath, and the other to have Crest breath."

"Whoever told you life was fair?"

I pressed my lips against hers again. She nibbled softly on my mouth, then ran her fingers through my hair. Then she stopped and looked at me. "I like the mussed look on you. You seem more approachable. Less Vogue-like."

"That's certainly a nice way to tell me that I look as though I just got out of bed."

"I think that look is quite attractive on you. Now what do you say about some breakfast?"

"What about the pillow fight? And the afterwards?"

"Rita, look, I'm really sorry, but I can't. I told you, I'm not into casual sex. I hardly know you. I like what I know of you, and I'm definitely attracted to you. But I'd rather not just jump your bones, and then deliver you up to your husband."

"I thought gay people were supposed to be promiscuous."

"Oh really?"

The sarcastic look on her face let me know I had just lost some of my hard-earned non-heterosexist points. To make amends, I said gently, "That's what I've always heard, anyway."

"I see."

"Oh God, there's that 'you're a heterosexist yuppie' insinuation again!" I pulled away from her embrace.

"Well, come on. That's a generalization if I ever heard one! Promiscuous people are promiscuous, whether they are gay or straight. Please tell me you realize that." She reached over to touch my arm.

I turned towards her again. "I do. I'm sorry. I'm just a sexually frustrated would-be lesbian. Here I am throwing myself at you, and you keep dropping me on the floor like I'm too hot to handle."

The look she gave me let me know how accurately I had described the situation.

"Let's go have breakfast. Then I'll take you home. Do you have a car?"

I nodded, embarrassed to tell her it was a BMW.

"Okay then. When you've finished explaining to Paul your intention to dramatically alter your life, then come on over and we'll talk. Does that sound reasonable?"

I nodded again, then said "I'm scared."

"You wouldn't be human, if you weren't." She paused, and looked thoughtful. "Why don't we go to breakfast first? How about Doogers?"

"Definitely not. Paul might be there. That's his favorite breakfast place in Cannon Beach."

"Okay, what about the Midtown Café?"

"Sure. I don't think I've ever been there."

"I haven't either, but I've heard it's very good."

"Well, let's go then."

We drove into town, and pulled into the parking lot of the Midtown Café. The dining room was nearly full. We sat down at a table, and started looking around at the décor, done in mostly primary colors. There were novelty salt and pepper shakers everywhere. Each table had a unique set. We checked out the specials on the board. I decided on the Amish oat pancakes and an orange juice. Beth went for the omelet and a latte. We split a mixed fruit scone. It all tasted deliciously homemade. We complimented the owner on her superb baking skills.

After a second cup of coffee, I snatched up the bill before Beth could protest. I plunked down enough money for our breakfasts and a tip, then we made our way back out to the camper. I looked up the road in the direction of my cottage, then said, "I can just walk the rest of the way from here. It might help if I had some time to think."

Beth squeezed my hand reassuringly. "Whatever you'd like."

I pulled it away abruptly, trying to ignore the fire her touch had ignited in my body. "No, on second thought, just take me home quickly. I need to talk to Paul now before I lose the momentum of my revelation."

Beth took my hand again, and looked into my eyes. Her concern warmed my heart. "Rita, you don't have to change your entire life today, you know. There's no expiration date on mid-life crises. You can take some time to think about it. How long are you two supposed to be staying here?"

"Another five days."

"Then what's the hurry? Think it over; talk to Paul.

He may be ready for a change too. He may want to rekindle the old flame."

I snatched my hand away again. It made me angry that she didn't seem to notice what the touch of her hand did to me. It angered me even more that the touch of my husband's hands had never done anything for me. "You don't get it, do you? There never was a flame in my heart for Paul. That's what I realized yesterday. I married him because he was a good catch. I didn't love him then, and I don't love him now. It's all been a huge farce."

"I'm sorry. That must be a truly painful realization.'

"Yes, it is. Could you take me home now before I start crying?"

"Sure. Do you want to ride in the back or up front with me?"

"I want to be with you, Beth." I said quietly, hoping she could hear the words my heart was screaming out. I really did want to be with her. Not just for a few minutes; not just a few hours, but forever. I couldn't stand the thought of being away from her for even a moment. Yet I knew that I couldn't be with her, until I was no longer with Paul. The break up with Paul had already taken place in my heart. It was merely perfunctory to follow it through with action.

She opened the passenger door for me, and gestured for me to board. "Then come on, Rita. Time's a-wasting. There are fears waiting to be conquered, and beaches yearning to be combed."

I climbed in and fastened my seatbelt. I looked out longingly in the direction of the beach. "Is that what you're going to do today?"

She put the truck in reverse, backed out of the driveway, then headed in the direction of my house. "Yes. I'm going to hang out on the beach and pretend I'm on vacation."

I felt cheated that I wouldn't be able to go with her. "Aren't you always on vacation?"

"Definitely not. Just more so than most people."

Her light banter was clashing wildly with the

typhoon that was thundering away in my heart. I began to panic at the thought of letting her out of my sight. "How will I know where you are when I'm finished talking to Paul?"

"I'll give you my cell phone number. You can reach me anywhere then."

She stopped at a stop sign and checked her mirrors for cars behind her. Then she quickly jotted down her phone number on the back of a map of her campground. She tore off that part of the paper and handed it to me. I slipped it into my jacket pocket. As she drove, I studied her every movement. I watched her hands as they operated the gearshift and adjusted the mirror on the side of the pickup. She turned on the radio, then got excited when she heard the song that was just starting.

"I love this song! This is a song I wish I had written. It's perfect. The music. The lyrics. The emotions. It's flawless, and I don't say that about just any song."

"What song is it?"

"It's sung by Bonnie Raitt, but I don't think she actually wrote it. It's called 'The Lonely One.'"

She turned the radio up louder and started singing out loud with it. Her voice blended beautifully with Bonnie's. When the song was over, she turned the radio back down and looked over at me. "Don't you just love that?"

"You're quite passionate about music, aren't you?"

"Yes, I am. I've always felt as though I should bleed musical notes when I cut myself. I can feel music coursing through my veins, so it's a surprise whenever blood comes out. For then I find that I too am merely a mortal, albeit a music loving one. But then every once in awhile someone writes a song that's so beautiful, so perfect, it makes me want to cry. Do you ever experience music in that way, Rita?"

"I think I used to, but it's been a long time since I allowed myself to feel anything that deeply. I envy your ability to embrace your emotions."

"It's not always a pleasant experience."

"Perhaps not, but I bet you never wonder if you're really alive."

She drove past my house, then turned off at the parking lot where we had sat and talked the night before. "I really like you, Rita. I hope things go all right today. I really hope you find what you're looking for."

"You make it sound as if I'll never see you again."

She reached over, and wrapped one of her warm hands around mine. "I don't mean for it to. I just wanted you to know that, well, that there's someone in the world who cares about what you're going through. Someone who supports you in your quest for a new life."

I basked in the warmth of her hand. I placed my other hand on top of hers for a moment, then decided I needed to go. "I really appreciate that. Listen, do you mind if I walk the rest of the way from here? I think I need to walk along the beach by myself for awhile."

"Knock yourself out. I'm going to hang out here for a minute or two. There are a few things I need to check under the hood. I'll probably head for the beach after that, but I'll take my phone with me in case you need to talk."

I leaned over and kissed her smooth cheek. "Thanks, you're sweet."

Chapter Six

I started walking down the beach with the intention of gathering my courage for my heart to heart talk with Paul. What happened instead is that I started crying and couldn't stop. I mourned the wasted years I'd spent being the woman everyone else wanted me to be. I grieved for the woman I had buried alive under a mountain of social acceptability. By the time I got to the cottage, I knew what I was going to tell Paul. As I walked up the steps leading to the house, I saw him through the front window. He was standing there in his bathrobe with the telephone in his hand. I heard his agitated tone, as I walked in the front door. He waved at me.

"Yes, I can see that's it's urgent, but I'm on vacation, Daryl. Can't you handle it?" There was a pause. "Okay, fine. Yes, I'll be there tonight. Can you at least pull everything together for me? Just leave the brief on my desk." Another long pause. "Yes, I appreciate that. Thank you, Daryl."

He hung up the phone, then turned to look at me. "That was Daryl. The Trumbel case has blown wide open. I'm afraid I'm going to have to go back. I'm really sorry about this. I'll leave you the beemer. I can rent a car. I know you've been looking forward to this vacation, Rita. I hope you'll be sensible and stay here for awhile. Enjoy the ocean for both of us."

I laughed to myself at his oratory. He didn't have a clue what was about to happen, and I sincerely doubted if he would care on anything more than a superficial level. I thought about telling him to go ahead and draw up the divorce papers, but I knew he wouldn't even hear me. Instead I said, "I understand, Paul. That case is important to your career. It's not a problem. I'll just stay here and rest. I may even stay a couple weeks or longer. Don't worry about me. I'll be just fine."

He looked at me as though he had expected me to protest. "Are you sure you're going to be all right?"

"Yes, quite sure. Really, don't worry. I'm fine. In fact, I'm looking forward to a nice long stay here by myself."

He shrugged. "Well, that's settled then. I'll stay until this evening, then drive back."

"No! I mean, there's no need for you to wait until tonight. You'll only wear yourself out. Why don't you go back as soon as you get ready? I can help you pack while you get dressed. I know this is important to you."

"If I didn't know better, I'd think you were trying to get rid of me."

I smiled at him. "I am."

He looked at me as though I'd lost my mind, then must've decided I was joking. "I'll get dressed then. Would you at least like to grab some breakfast at Doogers?"

"No, you go ahead, Paul. I'm not hungry."

"Fine."

He dressed while I packed his things. Within thirty minutes, the rental car was dropped off at our house, and he was gone. At first I felt giddy with the sense of freedom. Then I felt lonely. Then I just felt tired. I took a long bath, and decided to walk over to the restaurant to get a cup of coffee to wake me up. Even though I was feeling sleepy, I wasn't ready to go back to bed yet. I hoped Paul would be gone already from Doogers.

I put on a lavender print blouse and black knit slacks, then frowned at myself in the full-length mirror. How utterly boring I had become. I dug through some clothes Paul left here year around. I changed into a navy blue polo shirt of his, and my khaki chinos. The shirt was a little large on me, but not too bad. I was startled by the difference I saw in my own reflection. I looked as though I were ready for anything. I didn't know if it was the change of clothing, or a change in my attitude, but I suddenly felt stronger than I had in years.

I walked over to the restaurant, and started to enter when I saw Paul on the pay phone. His back was to me, and I almost walked right past him until I heard what he was saying.

"Yes, darling. That's right. I'll be there tonight. It worked. I'm free for the whole week." He paused. "No, I don't think she suspected a thing. She almost seemed glad to get rid of me. I think she'll enjoy the time alone. We're not used to being together all the time anyway. I'm not sure how we could have made it through a week of it." He laughed low and seductively into the receiver. "Yes, Maddie, and we can dine anywhere you want to tonight. See you soon, darling. I love you passionately, and I can't wait to hold you in my arms again. Bye."

He turned around, and almost passed by me, when he suddenly recognized me.

"Rita! Hi! I thought you weren't hungry. What were you doing standing there?"

"I   was   just   listening   to   your   telephone

conversation."

"Really?" His years as an attorney had paid off. He was able to stand there, looking me in the eye as though absolutely nothing was amiss.

"Yes, really. Just mail me the divorce papers, Paul. I won't contest it."

He put his hands on his hips and scowled at me as though I were a recalcitrant child. "What are you talking about?"

I slumped against the wall of the restaurant, and looked at the polished loafers on my husband's feet. "Paul, please, I'm not deaf, and I'm certainly not stupid. I heard you talking to Maddie. I never would've dreamed it would be her, but I guess it had to be someone, so why not her? She's certainly pretty enough."

Paul grabbed me by both arms, and tried to get me to look up at him. "Rita, it's not what you think."

I yanked away from his grasp, put my hands on my hips and defiantly asked, "How the hell do you know what I'm thinking, Paul?"

He staggered backwards, as though I had slugged him hard in the stomach. "I-you-I. You can't be serious about getting a divorce."

I glared at him. "I'm very serious."

"She doesn't mean anything to me."

"Neither do I. That's the whole problem. Nothing matters to you except your career. But it's okay, Paul. I don't really care. It just makes it that much easier for me. I was planning on asking for a divorce anyway."

"You don't mean that. You're just upset. Why don't we talk this over in my car?"

"Paul, I do mean it. I'm not upset. A little surprised, but that will pass. I realized yesterday that I never have loved you, and I assumed you didn't love me, so why should I be shocked that you're having an affair? Just have the papers drawn up, and I'll sign them. All I want is the cottage. You can have everything else."

"Look, Rita . . ."

"Good-bye, Paul. You're going to be late for your

dinner date."

I opened the door for him.   He walked out frowning. "We'll talk later."

"I'm sure we will. Good-bye. Tell Maddie I said 'Hello, and thanks.'"

"You're being cruel, Rita."   He looked at me pleadingly, a small pout beginning to form on his lips. But I knew that trick, and I wasn't about to fall for it this time.

"No, Paul, I'm just being Rita. For the first time in my life. Now go away, or I'll make a huge scene right here in front of God and everyone else."

I shut the door in his face, then entered the main dining room of the restaurant. I let the waitress seat me at a table, then fell to studying the menu. Maybe it was relief, or maybe it was shock, but I found that I couldn't remove the smile on my face.   I ordered a second breakfast, and ate with gusto, relishing the thought that my new life had begun. It had been much easier than I had dreamed it could be. Guilt would keep Paul from working too hard to keep the marriage together. He would handle the entire affair with aplomb. Of that I had no doubt.

When I had finished my breakfast and paid my bill, I smiled cheerily at my waitress, handed her a five-dollar tip, and then headed out the door. I decided to see if Beth was still parked in the lot above the cottage. I walked over there only to find an empty camper. I scanned the horizon expecting to see her figure leaning over her guitar somewhere, but she was nowhere in sight.

I walked back to the cottage and started packing up Paul's clothing. I took off the polo shirt I'd been wearing and threw it in the box with his other things. I found a tattered T-shirt I had used when we repainted our deck furniture last year. I put that on instead. I sat down next to the window, and stared out at the ocean. Even though the windows were closed, I could still hear the sound of the surf. I opened the windows to let in the morning breeze. The sounds of the waves soothed my tormented mind.

As I sat there, I thought I caught a few strains of music floating on the breeze. I wondered if that might be Beth singing, so I donned a windbreaker, and went out to comb the beach for the beachcomber. I found her sitting just below the house on the sand. She was playing her guitar and singing.

I stood there entranced by her form, her music, her indigo hair buffeted by the wind. I suddenly felt as though I were being handed another chance in life. A chance to do with it what I wished, rather than what everyone around me expected me to do. I walked up quietly behind her, and sat down just to the right of her. When she had finished playing, she turned and looked at me. She smiled at me, her eyes dancing with laughter.

"Do you live around here?"

"Yes, as a matter of fact, I do. I live in this house right above you. By myself."

"By yourself?" She looked somewhat surprised, but duly impressed.

"Yes, my husband has gone back to Portland to be with his girlfriend. He's going to draw up divorce papers for us, and I'm starting a new life as a beach bum."

"His girlfriend? Oh, I see."

"Do you now? What do you see?"

She looked intently at my face, as though she were studying each line, every nuance of expression. Finally she said, "I see a woman with fire in her eyes. A woman who has decided to own her feelings, to know herself, to provide a place for love to take root again in her heart."

"Really? All that? My, but aren't you a perceptive stranger?"

She smiled shyly at me. "It's a gift."

"No, Beth. You're the gift."

She reached out and squeezed my arm. Her touch brought tears to my eyes, for some reason. Perhaps it was because I knew it was sincere. Perhaps it was because it signified a new beginning for our relationship. We had weathered the first storm together. There would be many more no doubt, but we had survived the first one, and that was enough for the moment.

"Would you like to see where I live?" I gestured towards the house above us.

"I would like that very much. I don't suppose you have any coffee made."

"No, I had to go get some at Doogers. That's where I broke the news to Paul about our impending divorce."

I told her the story as we walked up the steps to the house. We went inside, and I made a pot of coffee. We sat on the floor and talked and laughed. We even cried together a few times. Hours passed quickly. In the early afternoon, we walked to the grocery store to buy some food for the cottage. We bought a couple turkey club sandwiches at the deli, then ate them outside on the benches where we had sat the day before. It was hard to believe that I had been so frightened by this beautiful lesbian guitar-player. We also bought some supplies to stock my refrigerator and pantry.

As we walked back home, she clasped the hand that wasn't carrying groceries. I squeezed her hand and laughed. "This feels so right to me. I feel as though I've known you for a thousand years."

Beth nodded. "Yeah, me too. It's the lesbian bonding thing, I think. We're good at projecting a long established sense of intimacy. We tend to substitute intensity for duration. It helps to speed things along."

"I see."

She grinned at me. "And just what is it you see, Rita?"

I looked at her and laughed. "I don't know. I just thought it was the thing to say."

She looked at me more seriously. "Do you understand though?"

"I think so. I've never had a lesbian friend before, so I'm not quite sure."

She gave my hand a squeeze. "It's okay. I can show you the ropes."

"I never doubted that for a moment."

I released her hand, then slipped my hand through the bend in her arm and snuggled up closer to her. I watched people's faces as we passed by. No one seemed to notice that we were two women walking along intimately joined together. Or if they noticed, they certainly didn't seem to care. I decided then and there that I had been right to settle in Cannon Beach. It was my kind of town.

Chapter Seven

When we got back to the cottage, we unloaded the groceries, then sat down for a cup of tea. The morning fog had burned off, and the sun was shining brightly. We decided to go for a walk on the beach. As we walked along, Beth kept her eyes on the beach mostly. Every once in awhile she would bend over and look closely at something in the sand. She picked up a sand dollar that was intact, except for the center, which looked as though it had been carefully removed. She found several more just like it. She looked at me with a frown on her face. I was beginning to realize that her frown was an indication that she was pondering something, rather than that she was upset.

"Now I wonder what causes that. Do the sand dollars come in with the tide, then get pecked at by the gulls?"

I shrugged, not having any particular insight into the lives of sand dollars and sea gulls.

"Hmm. What an odd thing life is. Life constantly feeding on life. I've thought about becoming a vegetarian several times because I didn't like the thought of eating living things. Then I realized that plants are living too, so what's the difference? I may yet though, because at least you can eat part of the plant without destroying or wasting the rest of it. You can't exactly eat the leg off a chicken, and expect it to continue thriving. Plants even do better when you prune them. Animals don't."

"My parents are vegetarian.   They are former

Seventh Day Adventists who retained their dietary habits."

"Did you rebel against them?"

"Not really. I still don't eat flesh foods when they're around. It was being around Paul that changed my eating habits. It's difficult to be a good hostess for a young lawyer who's making his way in society, without serving meat products. Of course, we served mainly seafood and poultry. I've never eaten much red meat. Perhaps that's one of the things I'll have to consider as I construct my new life."

"Well, you'll fit in well with the lesbian intellectuals if you become a vegetarian."

"My, but that does sound like a generalization."

"It does, but it's true. If you go to social gatherings sponsored by lesbians, there will be little if any meat at all. Now of course, if you're ever invited to a cook-out, then chances are, you've discovered some meat lovers."

"Somehow I'm getting the feeling that there's a whole world of things to learn about being lesbian."

"Yeah, there's another whole book of etiquette to memorize. Some of it overlaps with regular society. Some of it is very specific to our community."

"You'll have to fill me in, so I don't commit a faux pas."

"I'm afraid you may need to buy a book, if you wish to become the Emily Post of the lesbian community. I'm not very good at that kind of thing. That's one of the reasons I spend a lot of time alone. I'm not a very social creature. But I suppose I can give you one or two tips."

By that time we had reached the house again. We went in, and Beth sat down on the floor in the living room. Having worked up a thirst from our walk, I went to the kitchen and made us both some lemonade from the mix I had bought that morning. I handed my companion her glass, and sat down on the floor beside her. She was thumbing through a copy of Martha Stewart's *Living* magazine. She was chuckling at a photograph of Martha working outside.

"I take it you don't like Martha Stewart."

"I don't dislike her. I just have a hard time identifying with someone who puts on makeup to work in the yard."

I laughed at her, and myself as well. "Well, I have bad news for you because I put on make-up to work in the yard."

She shook her head and grinned at me. "I see." I smacked her with a throw pillow. She fell over to one side, and lay on the floor smiling at me. "Are you always this violent, or is it just because I'm lesbian?"

I leaned over her and looked into her eyes. "I think it's just that the sexual tension inside me gets to be too much sometimes. I have to release it somehow." She sat up again, and nodded at me. I got the feeling that she was guarding herself from me. But since the subject of sex had been brought up, I forged on. "When was the last time you had a lover?"

She looked out the window, clearly avoiding my gaze. "Nearly two years ago."

I reached over, and gently turned her face back towards me. "Are you serious?"

"Yes. I told you I'm not promiscuous."

"Promiscuous?   Hell, Beth, you're downright celibate! You mean to tell me you've gone two years without sex?"

She frowned, then shook her head at me. "No, I've gone two years without a lover. I have sex with myself. Don't you ever masturbate, Rita?"

"Oh do I ever! Paul is so predictable and boring in bed. I'm so glad I no longer have to endure our Sunday morning ritual. Sex without love is so banal."

She gave me a penetrating look. "Have you ever had sex with someone you loved?"

I looked at her, then shook my head slowly. "No, I don't suppose I ever have.   What an odd thing to realize at age thirty-five. It's pretty pathetic, I guess. What about you? Do you ever have sex without love?"

She shook her head. "No, the old libido doesn't seem to function until the heart has been engaged. I guess my heart is kind of like a clutch in that way. I can sit and idle for awhile, or even start out jerkily in first gear, but I just don't seem to get anywhere until my heart gets involved."

"That explains a lot."

"Yeah, I guess it does." She smiled at me tenderly. "I guess I'm not the best lesbian friend for you. Perhaps we should find some shameless lesbo hussy somewhere to bed you down."

"Am I that bad?"

"No, I don't mean for it to sound that way. It's just that, being with a woman isn't a novelty to me. I'm in no hurry. I like to savor those first stages of friendship before wading into deeper waters."

"But the way you talked when we first met . . ."

"Harmless banter. I was merely trying to wake you up a little bit. Maybe I was just coming out to you in a brusque way, just to get that part over with. I really hate getting acquainting with someone when I know for a fact they're assuming I'm heterosexual. It makes it so much more startling when the revelation comes later. By that time, I'm liable to lose the person to paranoia. I hate that sudden chilling of the atmosphere. I don't know how many times I've had women say to me, 'why didn't you tell me?' As though they had introduced themselves as 'Helen the heterosexual.'"

"Which is what I did, I suppose, by telling you that my husband and I were on vacation."

"Yeah, and that was fine. It let me know where you stood. That's probably part of the reason I came out to you so quickly. After I found you staring at me like you wanted to absorb me into your skin, I thought it might be best if I let you know where I was coming from. Then there would be no chance for you to accuse me of trying to seduce you. In a way I think I was trying to scare you off. I don't have enough emotional energy to deal with homophobic people. They make me too sad."

"I was a little put off by your bluntness at first. I felt as though you were testing me."

"I guess I was. I suppose that was kind of mean. I just didn't want you to think you had found a soul mate, only to later discover that I didn't share your obsession with the male species."

"Oh, but I did find a soul mate because I'm not obsessed with the male species."

"No?"

"No. I've tried to tell you that I was doing what everyone expected of me. For some bizarre reason, known only to the deities of introspection, I needed to meet a blue-eyed lesbian guitar player to make me realize that I no longer wanted that life. That I was willing to walk away from it all in order to find myself."

"It's strange sometimes to discover what each of us needs to reach that moment in time, when we're willing to discard everything to follow our personal truth. "

"What did it take for you?"

She was silent for a moment while she gathered her thoughts.

"It was a whole progression of events, but the trigger was a job I had. I worked very hard at it, just because that's the way I am. Whatever I do, I do it wholeheartedly. So here I was busting my ass for this company that I realized didn't give a flying fig about me or anyone else, including our customers. The bottom line was money. The top line was money. And every line in between was money, money, money. Finally I couldn't take it any more.

"It wasn't as though I thought that money shouldn't be important to the company. Obviously you can't stay in business if you don't realize that money is important. It was the comprehension that money was the only thing that was important. Employees were viewed as labor hours, customers as potential sales, etc., etc. There was no sense of value attached to the quality of care given to the customer. Customer service was merely a department in the company. It certainly wasn't an ethic. Job satisfaction was a joke. They offered minimal benefits and employed minimal employees. But I could go on and on, ranting and raving. I hate to bore you."

"No, I think it's interesting. I haven't had to deal with that sort of thing directly. Yet it's part of what made me so dissatisfied with my life with Paul. For him, the only thing that was important was his career. The money was there all along. He came from a moneyed family. So did I. Neither of us have ever wanted for anything material. But I found it wasn't enough. I wanted something more. When I saw you on the beach bearing your soul to the universe in a way I've never been able to, I suddenly knew what was missing in my life. I'm not sure what to call it. Communion with nature, maybe?"

"I'd call it attachment. I've read a lot of philosophical works over the years. One of the things I have come to realize is that the reason I can't embrace Buddhism is that it teaches us that the world we see is an illusion, and that all suffering arises from our desires and attachments to this illusory world. If we train ourselves to detach from the world around us, to let things pass us by without being affected by them, then we can minimize the amount of suffering we have to endure."

She looked at me to see if I were still with her, then continued.

"But I don't want to detach from this world, illusory or not. Desiring is part of being alive. So is suffering. Without desire, without suffering, there is no passion in life. When I think of all the works of creativity that have been birthed in the throes of desire and suffering, it makes me cringe to think that we should try to rise above these elements of our humanity. To detach ourselves from desire and suffering is to cut off the source of our creativity. If I cut off my creativity, then I might as well be dead. So for me, a life without passion is no life at all. It's death.

"I realize that I am a mere mortal, and that one day my body will die. That's okay. I don't mind letting go of the outer form. But I know there is something, Someone, deep inside of me who will continue on after my body is gone. That Someone is the one who cries over a perfect song. That Someone is the one who can write a song about desire and suffering because she has experienced it. She is the one who can watch a thousand sunsets, and never get tired of them. She is the one who loves what is inside a person, not what's on the outside. She is the one who refuses to be treated as a labor hour.

"When that Someone woke up in me, I found it impossible to let her go back to sleep again. I realized that I wanted to experience all the emotions inside of me, even the painful ones. I wanted to be attached to my body, my mind, my feelings. I wanted to live my life by my heart, not merely by my head. So I started selling all my possessions to save up for a camper and a life of relative freedom. I still have to work for a living at times, but I don't get too caught up in it. I just work, and earn enough money to move on again. In some ways, I think I've come closer to what the Buddhists would call being detached by allowing myself to attach to my inner world. Perhaps that's what they were trying to say all along. I don't know. Still I find myself rebelling against the idea that Nirvana is being able to get off the cycle of death and life. I like the idea of living and dying over and over again, a thousand times into eternity. I love the passions of life, both good and bad.

"I cry inside when an animal is struck by a car and killed, and yet I know it will return again to this world. But I still stop and mourn it's passing. I hurt when I think about animals killing each other, both human and otherwise, and yet I know it is all part of this thing called life. I'd like to make the universe a happy and cheerful place, where we're all loving and considerate of each other. Yet I know inside that the universe that exists is much more balanced and sane than the way I would have created it. Each of us just needs to do our part in making it as kind and considerate a world as we are capable of creating. It's a collective effort on the part of the whole universe."

I listened intently to her words, sensing the passionate soul who spoke them. I suddenly had this mental image of a little bird being released from its cage. That little bird was me. These were the thoughts and feelings I had been being bombarded with over the past couple days. They were the thoughts and feelings that had been cautiously tiptoeing around in the back alleyways of my mind for years. It had taken a lone guitar player on the beach to sing the lullaby that put my everyday sensibilities to sleep long enough for my eternal soul to wake up and say, *There's more to life than what's up there on the stage. Get out there and find out what it's all about.*

She sat up and looked at me. "So I guess you probably think I'm a real nut case now."

"On the contrary. You've just put into words all the nebulous ideas that have been floating around in my head for a long time. I had no idea anyone else felt the way I do. I have felt so alone, for so many years. So isolated, so insulated from it all. As I walked along the beach this morning thinking about how I was going to tell Paul I wanted a divorce, I embraced the grief I experienced. I found that it wasn't the marriage I was mourning so much, as it was the moments it had stolen from my life. I don't want the rest of my life to feel as trivial as the first part has. I want to live, really live. To embrace both pleasure and pain." I looked closely at her to see how she was taking all this. "You're such a gift to me, Beth. I wonder how long it would have taken me to wake up if I hadn't seen you down there on the beach."

"I think you saw me when you were ready. If you hadn't been ready for this metamorphosis, you wouldn't have been altered by my presence on the beach. It's not me who changed you, Rita. It's you."

"You're right, of course. But still. Thank you for being there. Thank you for following your dream, which led you here to Cannon Beach."

She smiled at me, and reached over to touch my cheek with the back of her hand. I leaned over to kiss her, passion spilling out of a heart that was full to the brim for the first time in my life. She kissed me tenderly, then held me against her chest. I listened to the sound of her heart beating, and realized that this was what was important in life. Moments like these when two people can look into each other's eyes and find common ground. Emotionally exhausted from our conversation, I fell into a relaxed sleep on her chest.

When I awoke it was dark. She was asleep too, her head resting against the couch. I eased myself up carefully, hoping not to wake her, but she stirred anyway. She looked around as though she were disoriented momentarily. "So what time is it? I'm ravenous."

I turned on a lamp, and stared at the tiny numbers on my watch. It's nine-thirty. Would you like for me to make some dinner for you?"

"We could make it together. What shall we have?"

"How about a pasta salad? That should be fairly quick. How are you with a knife?"

"Cautious."

We both laughed, and went into the kitchen. Aside from neither of us being accustomed to that kitchen, we worked well together. We bumped into each other a couple times trying to reach things. I liked it when that happened. I liked feeling her body press up against mine. I found myself looking over at her, watching her chop up vegetables and herbs as deftly as she played her guitar. Here was a woman who seemed to treat all of life like a poignant song.

When the salad was done, I stabbed some of it with a fork and held it out to her. "How does this taste?"

She stepped closer to me, and took a bite, holding my hand steady with hers. I felt a tingle of desire course through my hand. She looked at me as her lips slid off the fork. "Mm, that's perfect. Just the right blend of flavors, and colorful too. Martha Stewart would be proud."

I took a bite and said, "You're right. It is perfect. Shall we set the table?"

"No. I think we should stand here and eat from the bowl. What do you say, Ms. Stewart? Can you break away from convention long enough to try that?"

"Only if you let me feed it to you."

Her eyes sparkled with laughter. "You read my mind, Rita. Hand me a fork, and I'll see to it that you get some nourishment too."

I gave her a clean fork, then speared some more

salad. She stepped even closer to me, and took the food I was holding out for her. She chewed slowly, watching me with a glint in her eyes.

"Your eyes look green now. I thought they were blue."

"They change with whatever color shirt I'm wearing. Yesterday I had on a blue T-shirt. Today my shirt is green."

"Please don't ever wear red. That might prove to be unnerving."

She laughed. "Well, mostly they just alternate between different shades of blue, green, and gray. I've never known them to change to purple or red or brown."

"How convenient to have eyes that match your clothing."

"Isn't though?"

She fed me a forkful of pasta. I touched her hand lightly as I took in the food. I didn't really need to help her to aim; I just wanted to touch those wonderful hands. I found that I was beginning to be obsessed with them. I turned to get the napkin that was sitting on the counter. I dabbed my lips with it, while she brushed back a lock of hair that had fallen into my face. Then she slipped one hand into my hair, and turned my head to face hers. She gently kissed my forehead. That kiss seemed almost more sensual than the ones we had shared with our lips.

The sexual energy between us was increasing, yet it was also being shaped into something more personal, more intimate. I found myself feeling glad that we hadn't had sex the night before. It would have been more lust than anything else, lust and sexual experimentation. I wasn't sure what I wanted from this woman, but I knew that I wanted more than a one-night stand.

"I think I'd better go, Rita. It's getting late."

"Couldn't you stay? You don't really have to leave, do you?"

"I think I should."

"Don't you, aren't you feeling what's between us? Don't you care for me?"

She smiled slowly, thoughtfully. "You're growing

on me. But I don't want to rush it. We have all the time in the world now. Let's savor this feeling the way we've savored the taste of our pasta creation. There's no need to consume it all in one sitting."

Having said that, she kissed me carefully on the lips, then stepped back from our embrace.

"Don't you even want any more to eat?"

"Rita, there are a lot of things I want right now. But I'm willing to wait until the right time comes. As for food, I'll get a snack at the camper."

"But . . .?"

"Would you like to walk over with me to the truck? I'll drop you off here again on my way back to the campground."

"Yes, I'd like that. I don't want you wandering around on the beach alone."

"You might need your jacket. It's probably chilly out there by now."

"What about you?"

"I'll be all right, as long as you walk close to me."

She held open the door for me, waiting while I put on my windbreaker. I led the way out, locking the house behind us. We walked down to the beach, pausing a moment to listen to the pounding of the waves. The smell of salt water wafted on the night breezes, filling our senses with its fragrance. The stars that filled the sky faintly lighted the night. Most of the clouds that had been there earlier had floated out to sea, ready to return with the dawn. The moon was a beautiful silver crescent hung artfully above the nightscape. Its reflection was magnified on the water.

As I stood there pondering the vastness of the universe, Beth turned around to face me, and kissed me long and deep. Then she let go again reluctantly, and we started walking towards the camper.

"Are you sure you don't want to . . .?"

"Yes, Rita, I'm sure. There's something I need to do tonight. I'll see you in the morning though. Would you like to have breakfast together?"

"I'd love it. Shall I make it for us, or would you like to go to somewhere?"

"Why don't we have it at your place?"

"Okay. Breakfast at my place. What time?"

"Why don't you call me when you wake up?"

"I'll do that."

She opened the passenger door of the pickup, and I climbed in. She went around to the other side, got in, then just sat there staring out at the ocean for a few moments. She seemed to be lost in her own thoughts. I considered asking what she was thinking, but decided against it. I wasn't sure I wanted to know.

She started the engine, then drove away. When she pulled into my driveway, she got out of the cab, and came around to meet me as I was getting out. She took my hand and walked me to the door.

"You really don't have to go, you know."

"Are you afraid of being alone?"

"No, I hadn't even thought about that. I used to stay by myself all the time when Paul was away on business. Though come to think of it, he was probably just having a tryst with his secretary. It's so easy to kid yourself about stuff like that."

"Well, if you're not afraid to be alone, then I think it's best if you spend this first night by yourself. It will probably feel very different to you, since your husband won't be coming back this time. You need to do that for yourself. I'll see you in the morning."

She kissed my forehead again.

"I really want you, Beth."

"Not tonight, Rita. Don't forget there's the rest of your life to consider. Don't get sidetracked by falling in love with me."

"It may be too late for that."

"Don't do it, Rita. Tonight's your night. You can have anything you want."

"I want you."

"Okay, so maybe you can't have anything you want." She smiled a sly smile.

"What's the point of this newly found freedom, if I can't sleep with whomever I want?"

"You've gained your independence from your husband, and your past life as his wife. You can never gain independence from the responsibilities for your actions. They will follow you wherever you go."

I took this in, and nodded my head. "I'm sorry. I'm behaving like a spoiled child in a candy store." She squeezed my hand, then turned and walked briskly away.

Chapter Eight

Though I had closed the door behind her, I was unable to shut out the piercing desire I felt for her. Through the windowpane, I watched her blue-jeaned figure quickly retreating down the path to her camper. I wondered how I had gone so far through this life without realizing how easy it would be for me to love a woman. As I looked back over my life, I realized that I had always experienced pangs of desire towards women. I hadn't recognized them for what they were, because I hadn't experienced such emotions with my husband. How could I have acknowledged my desire for women, without also facing the lack of desire I had for Paul? I marveled at the soul's ability to take a person to another level of growth only when time was ripe for the harvest. I was able to experience love and passion towards Beth, because I was finally able to admit to myself that I had a loveless and passionless marriage. It was as simple as that.

I watched as the camper pulled away. I was puzzled to note that she had headed in the opposite direction I had expected her to go. She was heading away from the campground, rather than towards it. A moment of panic seized me as I pondered the possibility that she might be drifting away from me already. But remembering our date for breakfast, I assured myself that Beth was not the kind of woman to make a date, and then break it without a word.

As I turned away from the window, I noticed that

the cottage looked different to me. It looked as though it could use a facelift. It needed to stop looking as though it belonged to a yuppie heterosexual couple, and start looking as though it belonged to a single woman with her whole life ahead of her.

The first thing I did was to take down the pictures on the wall. They had come with the cottage, and Paul had liked them, so I had left them where they hung. But I had never cared for them particularly, so I decided to put something of my choosing up there. For now, I still had a joint checking account with Paul. I determined to use some of that money at the art galleries in town. On earlier visits to Cannon Beach, I had found several prints that I thought would look nice on the walls. But Paul had insisted that we didn't need anything else for the cottage.

The next thing I did was to rearrange the furniture. All the living room furniture had been arranged around the television. Paul's idea, of course. I decided to put the television in one of the back bedrooms, and make the living room a place where people could relax and get comfortable, without falling into the mindless habit of turning on the television whenever conversation lagged. That was Paul's way of dealing with intimacy issues. But I wanted to have a life, not to watch someone else's on a screen.

Tired from the rearranging, I sunk down into the cushions of the sofa. Suddenly I had the urge to take off my clothes and lounge around the house in my nakedness. That was a luxury I allowed myself only when Paul was out of town. I never did it when he was home for fear he would notice that I was bloated and premenstrual. Or worse, that he would decide he wanted to have sex. Once a week with him had been more than enough for me.

As I lay on the sofa, I began to massage my sagging stomach. I thought about doing some sit ups to work on remedying the loose skin, but I opted not to just yet. Instead I began to daydream about Beth. I saw her indigo hair dancing about in the wind, like a kite on a string. I imagined her playing her guitar, and staring out at the distant ships on the horizon.

My heart began to pound in my chest, as I envisioned her taking off her clothes, slowly, sensuously. I tried to imagine what her breasts would look like. Would they have pale areolas with small nipples? Or would they be dark and large and startling against her olive skin? Would her body be supple and rippling with muscles, or would it be soft and a little pudgy like mine? Would her pubic hair be indigo like the hair on her head? Would it match the way my light brown hair did? Would she have scars from her childhood, or from some accident or operation she hadn't told me about yet?

I felt the moisture building up between my legs. I reached down and began massaging myself. I held the vision of Beth playing the guitar on the beach, singing to the wind and waves, while I stroked my way into solitary ecstasy. I saw her eyes penetrating my soul, as I choked on the wave of desire that welled up inside my heart. I knew I was falling in love with this guitar-playing lesbian, and I also knew that she was right to try to stop me from doing it so soon. But I'd never been in love before, so I had no idea how to stop myself from falling headlong into the chasm. I wasn't sure I wanted to stop.

What was it Beth had said about experiencing all her emotions, including the painful ones? So maybe it was stupid to fall in love with a lesbian nomad. It had to be better than settling for a loveless marriage for fifteen years. Was it Tennyson who said, "It's better to have loved and lost, than never to have loved at all?" Now it was my turn to test that sentiment. Savoring such thoughts, I floated out onto the sea of dreams.

My first sensation the following morning was one of being cold. I had fallen asleep on the sofa, wearing nothing but a sheen of perspiration. I got up and headed for the shower. After I had warmed up under the steaming spray of water, I dug out some old blue jeans and a coral button-down blouse. I started to put on makeup, but decided against it. What was the point? Beth never wore any, so I was certain she wouldn't be repelled if I didn't. Who else's opinion did I care about? In a moment of impulse, I swept my entire collection of cosmetics into the trash can. I threw out my hair spray with it.

Starting today, I was a new woman. If I decided I wanted to wear makeup, then I would start all over again, picking and choosing as I went. If I decided I needed my hair to stop blowing in the wind, then I would put on a hat. I was a beachcomber. What beachcomber needs plastered down hair?

I knew I would have to replace some of my wardrobe, but I didn't feel right about throwing everything out at once. That was something I could do slowly but surely, passing on my old things to some charity. I had a couple pairs of blue jeans for working in the yard; that was a start. I found some tan sandals, and slipped my feet into them, surveying the overall effect in the full-length mirror. I approved of what I saw, then I dragged the heavy mirror into the closet and shut the door. No longer would it hold a center place in my life. I'd had enough of living my life according to appearances.

I went out to the living room, and pulled Beth's phone number out of the pocket of my t-shirt. Then I gathered up my discarded clothing, and threw it into the laundry hamper in the bathroom. It was only eight o'clock, but I figured Beth would be up by now. She had said that she usually didn't stay up late. However, when she answered the phone, I could tell that she had only just awakened.

"Hello?"

"Beth? Did I wake you?"

"No. I had to answer the phone anyway."

"What? Oh, for . . . you're funny."

"Thank you. I almost had you there, didn't I?"

"You did have me. Are you still interested in breakfast? Or should I call you for lunch?"

"No, I'm still interested. I just stayed up late last night."

"I thought you didn't usually do that."

"I don't. I was working on a new song, and I got carried away with my singing and playing. I don't think I hit the sack until after two."

"What's the song about?"

"You."

I paused while I absorbed this information. "Me?"

"You."

"Will you play it for me, or isn't it finished?"

"Oh, it's finished all right. It doesn't usually take very long to write a song, especially not when I'm feeling so inspired."

"I inspired you to write a song?"

"Yes. You sound surprised."

"No one has ever written me a song before."

"First time for everything."

I paused for a moment wondering where to go from here. Finally I ventured to ask, "When are you going to share it with me?"

"Well, it's about eight now. How about eight oh five?"

"Are you going to sing it over the phone, or do you just intend to drive fast?"

"Neither. I stayed all night at Tolvana Park, and now I'm walking down the beach towards your house."

"Are you serious?"

"Yeah. I can't play my guitar until all hours of the night in a campground. I had started writing the song in my head last night before I left you. So I decided to go back to the park to put it down on paper, and try it out. I ended up playing until nearly two. Then I was so sleepy I didn't feel like driving back across town to the campground, so I fell asleep. And here I am now at your door."

"What?"

"Come to the door and let me in, woman. It's cold out here!"

I rushed to the door and opened it to find Beth standing there with the phone pressed against her ear, and her guitar slung across her back. She turned off the phone, grinned at me, and said, "Aren't cell phones great?"

"You never cease to amaze me."

She grinned at me. "Hey, I didn't invent them. I

just happen to own one."

"Get in here."

She walked in, and leaned her guitar against the sofa. Before she could protest I put my arms around her neck and kissed her passionately.

When I abruptly stepped back away from her, she nearly stumbled into the wall. "Whoa! That was some kiss. Did you miss me that badly? I haven't been gone that long. How was your night?" She looked around the living room as she said this. "Never mind. I can see you were very busy. Is this a good sign?"

"What? That I rearranged my house to suit me? Yes, that is a good sign."

"Good for you. That's a great start. What next? Something for the walls perhaps? It looks like a little bare without the pictures. I take it you didn't like them."

"How observant of you. Yes, I would like to go to the art galleries today to look for something that pleases me. It wasn't that I disliked them so much; it's just that I wasn't wild about them. They came with the house."

"Mmm." She yawned, and stretched her arms above her head.

I smiled at her. "How do you like your eggs, sleepy head?"

"Over easy. Toast dark, but not charcoal. Coffee black."

"Coming right up."

"Want some help?"

"No, but you can play for me while I cook."

"Okay, but I don't want to play your song until you can pay close attention to it."

"That's fine. You can sit here, if that's comfortable enough." I pulled out one of the dining room chairs.

"Do you have any without arms? I would bang my guitar on those."

"Sure. The chairs on the side are armless."

"I'll get one. You cook. I'm very hungry."

Beth pulled up one of the other dining room chairs, and positioned herself and her guitar carefully, then began to play. She played some quiet instrumentals while I cooked. Within fifteen minutes, everything was done, and ready to be devoured. I set the table, then brought out the food.

She took a whiff of her plate, and smiled at me, "Smells delicious."

"Thank you. It's just eggs and toast. Not much to it." I sat down in my chair, while I watched my companion put her guitar aside, and pull her chair up to the table across from me.

"Well, I still appreciate your hard work. Thank you for inviting me over."

I reached over and put my hand on top of hers. "Thank you for suggesting we have breakfast together. I'm afraid I'm not quite sure how to go about dating a woman. Hell, I'm not sure I'd know how to go about dating a man any more. Not that I'm interested."

"No one's written a rule book yet, so I'm afraid we're on our own. But so far, you're doing fine."

I leaned back in my chair, and spread the red checked cloth napkin on my lap. "So, are you interested in accompanying me to the art galleries today?"

"Sure. I've been to most of the ones here. I like their selection. There are lots of good artists in this area. Do you have any idea what you want?"

"Actually I do. There are several Steve Hanks paintings I've been admiring for years now. I just never dreamed of having a place to put them. Now I have an entire house to decorate according to my own tastes."

Beth's face lit up at the mention of Steve Hanks. "Hey, isn't that the guy who does those beautiful watercolors? I love what he does with light. If I had any walls, I'd definitely hang his works on them. You have excellent taste. Are there any in particular you have in mind?"

"Yes, for the bathroom I want either the one with a woman lying naked beside a tiled bathtub, or the one of the woman taking a shower. I can't remember what they're called, but I'll tell you my heart almost stopped the first time I laid on eyes on them. For the den I'd like the one with the two cats on the bookshelf. I think that one is called "Bookends." Then for the living room I want to put up the woman who is standing there staring out to sea. There's another one I like of a woman leaning against a door post. I'll have to look around some more to figure out which other ones I want, and which are readily available."

"Sounds like you were a woman just waiting for the right conditions to blossom."

I beamed at her assessment of my progress. "I do believe I was."

We ate our food in silence for several minutes, then Beth asked, "Do you like cats?"

"Yes, I do. I have been thinking about acquiring a couple, now that I don't have to worry about Paul. He's allergic to cats, or so he says. I don't know if he's really allergic, or if he just doesn't like them. You don't happen to know where the nearest animal shelter is?"

"I don't, but I do know of some people who are staying at the campground that have a new litter of kittens. I'm sure the owners would let you pick out a couple, if you're willing to wait until they're weaned. They're about six weeks old, I think."

"But if they're at the campground, doesn't that mean they'll be leaving soon?"

"No, they told me that they usually come this time of year, and stay for a month or two, until it starts getting too cold and dreary for them. We'll have to check with them, but they'll probably be willing to give them up in a couple weeks."

"That's perfect. They should be ready for me about the time I'm ready for them. I'll have to go over there and see what I think."

We had finished eating, and were clearing away the plates when Beth said, "I can wash the dishes."

"No, don't bother. Let me get them. You can play me another song. Is that okay?"

"Sure. I'll need some water though, if I'm going to sing too. Singing makes me thirsty."

"I'm sorry I did think to offer it to you before breakfast."

"Not a problem. I'm not sure my voice was ready to start singing that early."

She played while I washed the dishes and cleaned up the kitchen. Then we got in the BMW, and headed down the street to the shops in town. I went first to Haystack Gallery, where I knew they had a good selection of Steve Hanks prints. I was able to secure almost all the pictures I had picked out in my head. I found a couple others by the same artist that fit in perfectly with my living room, both in style and colors. I especially liked one called "Sense of Belonging." The cool greens and blues matched the drapes in the living room; and the title of the work matched my newly found feelings about this town and this house. By the time I was finished, I had nearly wiped them out of Steve Hanks works, and turned my house into a private gallery in his honor.

When the last picture was hung and straightened to my satisfaction, Beth asked, "Would you like to go see the kittens now?"

I nodded my head and suggested that we grab a bite of lunch first. I got out the pasta salad again, and said, "I hope you don't mind leftovers. We made an awful lot last night, and you ate only two bites." I glared at her daring to turn up her nose at the pasta.

She smiled sheepishly and said, "Sorry. I was afraid I wasn't going to be able to leave at all, if I had stayed a moment longer. I really thought you needed your house to yourself, at least for the first night."

"Does that mean you'll stay tonight?"

She held her hands out as though to ward me off. "Slow down, Rita. Let's take this moment by moment, shall we?"

I slipped between her outstretched arms, which then encircled me. I kissed her lips softly, and whispered huskily, "Only if I must. I'm afraid that I realized last night that I'm falling for you rather quickly. But I'm a mature woman. I can live with the consequences, even if it means crying myself to sleep every night."

She shook her head slowly. The compassion in her eyes filled my heart with warmth. "That sounds awfully lonely. Did you cry last night?"

"No, actually, I rearranged the house, then fell asleep on the sofa."

"Bed too big?"

"No, bed too far away from tired woman." I smiled at her, hoping she wouldn't ask any more questions about my evening alone. It would have been rather embarrassing to admit to her that I had fantasized about her while masturbating.

Fortunately all she said was, "Ah, well, let me at that pasta. I'm ravenous. Shopping for art makes me hungry."

We devoured the pasta, then got into the camper and drove over to see the litter. I talked to the owners about claiming some of the kittens. They told me I could have whichever ones I wanted. No one else had acted interested yet, so I had the pick of the litter. I chose a bouncy, fluffy gray one, and a shy white one with a black goatee.

We stayed and watched them for awhile, before heading back to my house. I encouraged Beth to tell the campground host that she wouldn't be back for awhile. I figured if she wouldn't sleep with me in the house, she could at least park her camper in my yard, and save herself a few dollars. I made up my mind to give her a key, so she could get into the house to use the bathroom any time she wanted.

After we left the kittens, we drove back to the cottage, and went for a walk along the beach. We held hands as we walked. I caught a few people doing a double take, but no one seemed disturbed that we were a lesbian couple. That was the first time I actually admitted it to myself that I was a lesbian. I tried the label on for size, and decided I liked the way it fit. I did a mental twirl, looking at myself from all angles. Rita. Lesbian. Hmm. Yes, it was a perfect fit. I decided to take it home with me.

Chapter Nine

When we got back to the house, I noticed Beth's guitar in the corner, and realized that she had not yet sung her new song for me. I mentioned it to her, and she smiled that enigmatic smile of hers. All she said was "later." So I dropped the subject, and talked to her about having a house key to get into the house at night. She nodded, and thanked me for my generosity. I let her know that if she wanted to sleep in the house she was welcome to do that too. She leaned over and hugged me.

"I want you to have the time and the space to discover who Rita is. You went a long way towards that last night, what with rearranging your house, and removing things that didn't fit your tastes. I was amazed this morning when I walked in. The whole house seemed to be alive with possibilities and new hope. It felt really good. You've grown a lot in a very short time. You should be proud of yourself."

We walked over to the couch and sat down. "I am proud of myself. It felt great to make those changes. The next thing I want to do is to get rid of my old bed. I think I'd like to get a futon. I've wanted one for a long time, but Paul wasn't interested in anything except a traditional king size bed. I think he wanted the bed to be big enough so we wouldn't have to bump into each other during the night. Sometimes I can't imagine why it took me so long to read the signs. I've been so naive."

"Don't be too hard on yourself. We all see what we wish to see, and that rarely corresponds with what is really there."

"I hope you're not trying to tell me politely that I'm reading more into your actions than what is there."

"I'm talking about you and Paul. Let's put that relationship to rest first. Find out who you are; then we can find out if there is an 'us' in the future. I'm willing to be patient, but I'm worried about you. Are you willing to be take your journey alone?"

"I'm quite willing to embark on this journey of self discovery without anyone else's assistance. What I'm not willing to do, is to miss out on this opportunity to get to know you. I find you fascinating, Beth, and if you slip away before I have even begun to love you, well that would be very hard. You said it yourself; I have the rest of my life. That goes for the discovery of myself too. I don't have to do it all overnight; and I don't have to do it without anyone else in my life. You're here now, and you may not be here a week from now."

We both stopped talking for several minutes, lost in our own thoughts. Beth broke the silence first.

"How about a date tonight? May I buy you pizza for dinner? There's a great pizza place downtown. It's called Fultano's. It's not exactly a romantic dining experience, but the food is sure good. What do you say?"

"Sure, let me grab my purse and jacket."

We decided to walk downtown via Hemlock Street. I was beginning to realize that I would not have a great need for a car, while living in Cannon Beach. A thought occurred to me so suddenly that it burst out of my head before I had time to think it through. "I think I might buy a bicycle. I haven't ridden for years, but in this area, I think it would be a fun thing to do. I could ride on the beach, or into town. You hardly even need a car around here."

Beth nodded in agreement. "Are you going to ask for the BMW?"

"I'm not sure. It's a nice car, but the insurance is a bit steep. Plus, it reeks of yuppie status symbol. If I keep either of our cars, I think it will be the Volvo. But I'm not sure I can afford even that one right away. I've got to start thinking about what I'm going to do for a living. I'd like to work in one of the art galleries around here, but I don't know the first thing about getting a job in a place like that."

"Just go talk to the owners, and tell them about yourself. You have a great eye for decorating, and good taste in art. I think you'd be a real asset to them."

"You really think so?"

"I do."

"Well, maybe I'll do that, but not tomorrow.

Tomorrow I would like to look for a new bed. Are you interested in helping me disassemble the one in the master bedroom? I don't think I can manage it by myself."

"Sure. We can work on that after dinner."

We entered Fultano's pizza, and placed our order. We sat down with our glasses of beer, and waited for our pizza to show up. It wasn't very crowded yet. We had gotten in before the dinner rush. We made small talk mostly, not wanting to be overheard. The tables there were pretty close together, making it difficult to have an intimate dinner. When the pizza arrived, however, it more than made up for the pizza parlor atmosphere. We settled into a concentrated attack on the sumptuous fare.

We decided to walk home along the beach. As we neared Haystack Rock, we encountered a dozen or so people wading around in the tide pools. Some were climbing around on the rocks, while others were looking at the colorful starfish and anemones that had attached themselves to the moist rocks, while they waited for the tide to return. One woman was prodding at a starfish with a stick. She seemed to be trying to get it to release itself from the rock it was attached to. We watched her for a few seconds from afar, then Beth walked over to her, and said, "Excuse me, but I work for the Oregon State Department of Parks and Recreation, and I'm here to tell you that you must stop attacking that starfish."

The woman looked startled; then she got angry. "I'm not attacking it! I was only trying to see how hard it would be to get it to let go of the rock."

"That's exactly my point, ma'am. You have to push very hard, enough to harm the creature. This is a protected habitat, and what you are doing is very illegal. Now I can fine you, if you persist in tormenting it, or you can leave it alone. Take your pick." Beth stood her ground, hands on hips, exuding authority.

Disgusted, the woman threw her stick down and stomped off, mumbling to her husband. Beth came back over to me and merely smiled. I laughed to myself. "The Oregon State Department of Parks and Recreation, huh?"

She laughed quietly. "Well, it worked, didn't it? Somehow I had the feeling that only a threat would get her to stop harassing that poor thing. What the hell was she thinking, anyway? How would she like it if someone were trying to physically pry her away from her shelter with a big club? People just don't think before they mess with wildlife."

The evening air was beginning to cool down. I wrapped my jacket tightly around my body. Beth shifted her focus towards me. "Are you cold?"

When I nodded, she put her arm around me, and pulled me close to her side. Even though she didn't have a jacket on, I could feel warmth radiating from her body.

"Don't you ever get cold?"

"Sometimes. I'm usually pretty warm-natured though."

"Must be nice."

"It comes in handy when you live your life in campgrounds."

"Do you think you'll ever settle down?"

"I don't know. I suppose so, when I find a good enough reason to, or I get tired of moving."

I nodded, hoping that she would decide that I was a good enough reason to settle in Cannon Beach. Changing the subject, I asked, "Do you really think I might be able to get a job at an art gallery?"

"If the owners of those places have any sense whatsoever, they'll snatch you up in an instant. Of course I have no idea whether anybody is hiring right now, but there's only one way to find out." As we climbed up the steps that led to the cottage, Beth asked, "Are you ready for your moonlight serenade?"

"If you're ready to serenade me. I could listen to you all day and all night. Have you ever made any recordings?"

"I've got several really bad tapes of me singing."

"How could they be bad if you're singing on them?"

"They're amateur jobs, made with a jam box, that's how."

"Would you let me borrow one?"

She hesitated, as though she were debating how to answer my question. "Do you have a dual tape deck on your stereo?"

"I think the one in the cottage has one. I'll check in a minute." I opened the door, and walked over to the stereo. "Yes, it does. Does that mean we can make copies of them?"

She smiled at me, and shook her head. "They're not that great, believe me, so don't get your hopes up."

"I'll try not. You just bring me the tapes, and let me worry about whether they're up to snuff. Okay?"

She sat down on the couch. "Fair enough. I'll get them for you later." I watched her as she picked up her guitar to play. I loved the way she walked, and the way she talked. I loved the way she would flick her hair over her shoulder with a barely perceptible motion. I suddenly had an overwhelming desire to brush her beautiful long black hair, but I didn't know what she would think of that.

"Do you have any Indian blood in you? I mean, Native American Indian."

"Yes, I do. Not a lot, though. I'm part Iroquois. I think it only shows in my hair."

"Definitely your hair, but also your cheek bones. You have beautiful facial structure. You have the kind of face that will remain striking even into old age."

She looked at me with a puzzled look, then nodded. "Thank you, Elizabeth Arden."

"No really. You think I'm being sentimental, but I mean it. That's something I can tell about people. I spent enough time reading those stupid glamour magazines to have learned a little something."

"I believe you, Rita. It's just not something that I worry about. It's the inside of a person that matters to me. Looks fade, or get destroyed in a fire or automobile accident. What then? It's the beauty of the soul that doesn't fade. In fact, it grows stronger the older you get. It's the only thing about us that does. I guess that's because as the beauty of the body fades, it unveils the beauty of the soul."

"You are such an amazing person, Beth."

"We all are, Rita. Some of us just don't know it yet. Those are the ones who get caught up in the rat race and the games. But it's not worth it. None of it."

"How did you get so wise at such a young age?"

She laughed out loud. "I don't know that I am wise. I still feel as though I'm a small child, just learning to walk. But what I have learned so far, I've learned by allowing myself to become attached to this world, to truly experience it with every fiber of my being. I've learned it by listening to my own heart when it beats in the stillness of the night."

I sat down next to her on the couch. "I love you, Beth. I know I haven't known you long, but I still love you. You have the most beautiful soul I've ever encountered. I feel so lucky to have met you."

"Remember what I told you about my being a mirror?"

"Yes, I do."

"What you see when you look at me is what you are."

"But . . ."

She put her hand on my chin and gently turned my face towards her. "When you look at me and see a beautiful soul, it's because you have clarity of soul yourself. You cannot recognize the beauty of a soul without possessing it yourself, Rita. You, too, have a beautiful soul. I admit that I didn't see it at first. I was too annoyed at having been interrupted while I was playing. My vision was temporarily clouded by my immediate discomfort. Thanks for being patient with me, and for opening your heart to me. I was slow to see you for who you are. I kept tripping over your apparent yuppiness. That is a shortcoming I need to overcome, a prejudice towards the rich and glamorous. But I'm working on that; and meeting you has definitely helped me to see that rich people have souls too."

I placed my hand on hers, then pulled her hand down, holding it in my lap. "I'm just beginning to find mine, thanks to you."

"No, Rita. It's thanks to you. I did nothing. Now for your song, are you ready?"

I nodded eagerly, not bothering to conceal my excitement.

She pulled her hand away, then shifted in her seat beside me so she was facing me, more or less. "You've got to realize that I used a bit of poetic license. This won't be completely accurate in every detail. Understand?"

"Yes, I think so."

I was a little disappointed when she started playing a fairly loud tune. I had rather hoped it would be a quiet love song. But as I listened to the words, I began to feel the power of her singing. It was so beautiful I wanted to cry. She was singing about my life. She had captured my tears in a bottle, and presented them to me through the words of her song.

> Sometimes it gets so lonely,
> Living in this big old house of mine.
> It seems like such a shame.
> Living in the city isn't
> what people told me it would be.
> No one knows my name.
>
> I met a man and married,
> when I was just fifteen years old.
> I thought I was in love.
> Well, I don't know what happened
> He tells me that he loves me,
> But it's just not enough.
>
> Here I am once again
> Crying in the night.
> Here I am once again
> Waiting for morning light.
>
> I met a woman last week,
> And though I barely knew her name,

We talked most of the night.
She seemed to understand
the deepest feelings within me.
As I thought she might.

So unexpectedly,
I felt myself falling in love.
Could it be true?
If only I could be sure,
then I would give myself to her.
If I only knew.

But here I am once again
Crying in the night.
Here I am once again
Waiting for morning light.

Here I am once again
Crying in the night.
Here I am once again
Waiting for morning light.

Chapter Ten

I didn't realize until she had finished singing, that tears were rolling down my face. When she stopped playing I felt my chest tighten, and I began crying harder than I'd ever cried in my life. My body was racked by the powerful sobs coming from my torn and tattered heart. I couldn't dam the flow of anguish and relief, as it gushed from my body through my tears. Beth put her guitar aside, and encompassed me in her strong arms.

Through my tears I managed to whisper, "Oh God, Beth. I feel so naked."

"Newborns are always naked, Rita. Welcome to the world of conscious living. Your soul has been born anew."

She patiently held me until the sobbing gave way to exhaustion. Then she lay back on the couch, positioning me on top of her body. She stroked my hair, and kissed the top of my head. I immediately relaxed in her embrace and fell asleep. When I awoke an hour later, Beth was still awake beneath me.

"Are you awake, Rita?" She whispered.

"Yes, do you need to get up?"

"I do. I have a cramp in my leg."

I sat up as quickly as I could. I felt as though I'd been drugged; I was so sluggish.

"Why didn't you wake me? How long have you been cramping?"

"I don't know. Awhile. I'm all right. It's just a leg cramp." She sat up gingerly, rubbing her leg.

"Well, at least let me massage it." I tried to massage the calf muscle, but it was hard to get at through the thick denim material of her jeans. "Wait. Let me get you a pair of shorts to wear, so I can really work on it."

Beth frowned at me. "I'll just remove my jeans. I could never fit into your clothes."

"You could wear some of Paul's, I bet. I have his stuff packed up, but it's still in the closet in there."

"Thanks, but I'm okay."

She pulled off her jeans cautiously, trying not to make her leg hurt worse.

When I looked at her bare leg, I could see the knot beneath her skin. "Oh my God, Beth. I wish you would have awakened me. That must really hurt." I began massaging her, gently first, then more vigorously as the knotted muscle began to unravel under my care. "I should get you some Ibuprofen. That will help your muscles to relax."

"Oh sure. First you get me to take my pants off, and now you want me to take drugs to relax. See how you are." She winked at me, as I got up and carefully stretched her leg out on the couch where I had been sitting. I dug around in my purse for my pill box. There were two left, so I dumped them into my hand, and went to get her a glass of water.

I handed her both the pills and the glass. "Here you

go. These should help. I'm going to work on it some more, but we need to get this into your bloodstream in the meantime."

Beth gulped down the pills and the contents of the glass. I sat back down and began to work on her leg some more. After about five minutes of massaging, I asked, "Is it feeling any better?"

"Oh definitely." She didn't move her leg, so I assumed she wasn't tired of my rubbing. I found my hands wandering farther and farther from the injured muscle. As my hands began to tire from the work of massaging, I began merely stroking her leg. She didn't seem to mind, so I kept on. She leaned back on the sofa and closed her eyes. I didn't think she was falling asleep, but I wasn't certain. I kept stroking her legs, first one, then the other. I gave her a brief foot massage, playing with the soft spots between her toes. Without flinching, she opened her eyes just long enough to say, "That really tickles."

"I'm sorry. You must have incredible self-control. If you had tickled my feet, I would have been flailing trying to get away."

I decided to play a game to see how self-controlled she really was. I started to stroke farther up her legs, first around her knees; later working my way up her thighs. She lay there motionless, eyes closed. My hands moved up to her hips. When I rubbed her hips, her T-shirt shifted enough for me to catch a glimpse of her panties. I could barely see her dark pubic hair through the white cotton underwear she wore. *Indigo. I bet it's indigo*, I thought to myself.

I wondered how far she would let me go before she stopped me. I kept massaging and rubbing her. I circumvented her pubic triangle, and started to work on her belly. As I did so, the material of her shirt kept moving up and down with my motions, according me sneak previews of her lightly tanned skin. Finally I decided to risk it all, and started massaging her beneath her shirt. She didn't move. I rubbed her bare stomach, discovering that it was taut and strong. I rubbed her sides, and marveled at the massive rib cage that housed her powerful lungs.

Hardly daring to breathe, I brushed her soft breast just barely; then did it again. Still no movement. No motion signaling me to stop. Her eyes were shut in deep relaxation. I hoped she wasn't asleep. I would be too embarrassed if I discovered that I had been taking advantage of a sleeping woman. I brushed her soft breasts again slowly, and didn't pull away. I wrapped one hand around each of them and kneaded them gently. She breathed deeply, but not heavily enough for sleep. She was awake, and so were her nipples.

Overwhelmed by my desire to view these wonderfully soft breasts I was kneading, I pulled her shirt up a little. Finally she opened her eyes at looked at me. "Need some help?" With just those three words, she leaned up, and quickly popped her shirt over her head in one practiced motion. I nearly gasped as I laid eyes on her exquisite beauty. Her nipples were dark, yet small and shy. They were definitely awake, but they kept threatening to withdraw if I didn't keep touching them.

I stroked her broad shoulders, massaging the powerful muscles that must've been gained through long hours of holding up a guitar. I leaned over and kissed her stomach. Then paused to relish the moment before my mouth surrounded her breast. What a splendor I had been missing all these years. What a delight to the senses. It was a wondrous moment to remember. The softness of her skin, the sweet clean smell of her body. My lips touched her breast, triggering a tingling sensation that started in my mouth and spread throughout my body. I couldn't believe I had waited thirty-five years for this experience. Suddenly for the first time in my life, I knew what it was to experience real sexual passion. I understood everything in that single moment in time. All the love songs, the poetry, the sad movies, everything. I was experiencing both the love and the desire that had been the backdrop for these things. Where had I been all my life? What had I been doing with Paul?

Beth squirmed a little as my mouth captured her

breast. She opened her eyes to look at me again. I smiled sideways at her, not willing to remove my mouth from her breast. She smiled a slow, seductive smile, then closed her eyes again. I reached out and touched her cheek. She turned her head, and kissed my fingertips, then engulfed my fingers in her soft, wet mouth. She moved them in and out of her mouth rhythmically, increasing the voltage on the current that was coursing through my veins.

She reached down and stroked my hair as it lay plastered against her chest. Then she said in a playful, yet seductive, tone, "One of us is rather overdressed here." With that remark, I sat up and looked directly into her eyes. There was that Mona Lisa smile again. Only this time I knew what she was thinking. She wanted me. I could see the desire in her eyes. I could feel the flames flicking around my body, just waiting to consume me. The hair on my arms stood on end.

She unbuttoned my blouse, while I reached up to undo my bra. As the silky material of my top brushed across my skin, I shivered. I had no idea desire could be this palpable. I stood up and unzipped my blue jeans, and slid them down my legs. I stepped out of them, then pulled my panties off, and flipped them over the back of the couch. Beth chuckled deeply in her throat. It sounded almost like a growl.

I looked down at her underwear. She followed my gaze, then nodded. I reached out and began sliding them slowly down over her hips. She wriggled out of them, then pulled me down on top of her. I kissed her breasts. She kissed my hair, then began to fondle my breasts. She gently teased them into an aroused state. She leaned forward and bit into my neck. Not enough to inflict pain, just enough to let me know how hungry she was for me.

She stroked my hips and thighs, then ventured into my forest of pubic hair. She braved the wilds there, and discovered hidden springs. Springs that only I had known existed. They had never revealed themselves to Paul. But they not only revealed themselves to Beth; they flooded their banks, and threatened to wash us both away in the torrent. I felt the perspiration dribbling down the back of my neck, and along my spine. As she bravely plunged into the forest, I gasped in pleasure at all the delights she found there.

She growled at me, and made me feel as though I were a wild animal. I suddenly wanted to run naked and free through the countryside. I wanted her to make love to me beneath every tree, beside every stream. I knew no sense of shame. I knew no sense of boundaries between myself and this woman inside me. I shuddered violently in orgiastic summation.

I tried to rest against her, thinking my passion had reached its limits. But she knew the power that resided in her hands. I convulsed again, as her nimble fingers strummed the nerves of my body. I felt the music in her hands. It flowed from her fingers into my senses. It was the music of our passion, the passion shared between two living souls, joined together as one. I rested for a moment against her chest. I was tired, but I was also very aroused. I wanted to touch her soul with the same intensity with which she had touched mine.

I began licking her nipples. Then I kissed her passionately on the mouth, and on her neck. I stroked her stomach, then moved down to the indigo fur that covered the entryway to her sacred dwelling place. I let my fingers bounce around in the soft springiness of her pubic hair. I felt the dampness that was leaking out from her body. Then I heard her voice calling me as if from faraway. "Wait, Rita. I forgot."

I sat up a bit, rather startled by this strange interruption. "What did you forget?"

She whispered, "Have you ever been with anyone besides Paul?"

I shook my head vigorously, looking at her in confusion. She was barely able to talk, as I continued probing her body, searching for the key that would grant me access to her hidden realms. "Did you always use condoms?"

"Yes, Beth, neither of us wanted kids. Why are you

asking me these questions now?"

She sat up halfway. "I forgot. I always check beforehand. It's been so long, and you caught me unawares. I have some dental dams and latex gloves in the camper. I thought I would have a chance to get them, if we needed them. But if you're clean, we should be okay. I've always practiced safe sex. I know I don't have anything."

I looked at her and laughed. She realized how ridiculous she appeared to me and laughed too. "Hey, you can't be too careful these days."

"Well, don't worry about me. Paul and I practiced sanitized sexuality. He may have been sleeping around; but I wasn't, and he never got near me without a barrier."

She nodded her head and leaned back. "Okay." She closed her eyes again, and relaxed under my touch. I tried to refocus my attention on the power I felt surging through my hands. I found her body pliant, yielding to my every tactile suggestion. Suddenly I felt the cone of her volcano rising beneath my fingers. When she erupted, it seemed as though the whole house reverberated with the strength of the shock waves. Lava poured out from the hot center of her body. When I tried to make it happen again, she clasped my hand, and said, "No, not again. That was too big. There won't be another."

She collapsed beneath me. Our bodies were floating in a pool of hot liquid. The perspiration poured off my head and back. Our bodies stuck together with the suction that had formed between them. I found that my legs were annealed to hers. We laughed as we peeled our bodies away. The rending was both physical and spiritual. We had been one in body, soul, and mind. We were two again, and I wanted to cry. I wanted to return to our united state, but I knew it was over for the time being.

I had an inexplicable desire to smoke a cigarette, something I hadn't done in ten years. I looked at Beth who was trying to get her eyes open. I smiled at her confusion.

"So was it good for you?"

She snorted.

Chapter Eleven

After a few minutes respite, Beth said, "I am so hot, I'm about to catch this sofa on fire! Can I use your shower to get cooled off?"

"Of course. Go right ahead."

I stood up reluctantly, not wanting to let her escape. I wished that we had been able to hang onto that moment forever. It didn't seem quite right to me that it should pass away so quickly. It would last no longer than any of my most mundane experiences; and yet it had been the most sublime moment, the most earth-shattering experience of my life. I wondered what Beth thought about it. Had it been just another night of good lesbian sex for her? Or was she as changed as I was? I pondered these thoughts while she showered. When she returned, I was almost afraid of what I might see in her eyes. But when I finally braved a glance, I found tenderness and caring.

"It's getting late. I should probably go out to the camper now."

"Can't you spend the night in here?"

She shook her head. "You still need time for yourself. To think things through. To make this house your own. I'll be right outside, and I'll be thinking about you. But I don't want to stay inside with you, crowding out your thoughts. You have a lot of emotions to process. A lot of plans to make. I'm not about to provide you with an excuse not to deal with all that. Good-night, Rita."

She put her arms around me, and kissed me gently. "I'll see you tomorrow, if that's what you want. But remember, if you want to be alone, then that's all right with me too. I won't come in here until you let me know you're ready for company. Do you understand why I'm doing this?"

"Sort of, but not really."

She released me and took a step backwards. She lifted my chin, making me look into her eyes. "Then just trust me."

I nodded. "Okay. Good-night, Beth."

She smiled at me, then grabbed her guitar and headed out the door. I handed her the house key so she could get in to use the restroom during the night.

"Thanks, Rita."

As I locked the door behind her, I felt the atmosphere in the house change. I suddenly felt alone. Really alone. No husband to come home from a business trip. No one filling up the house with the sounds of the television. No lover to hold me in the middle of the night. I opened a window, and stood before it listening to the ocean below. The sound of the waves crashing on the beach soothed me, washed me clean of self-pity. I began to realize that I wasn't alone; I was experiencing solitude.

It was true that I no longer had a man to care for me. I laughed to myself, realizing how foolish I had been to think Paul had ever really cared about me. We had both been young when we got married, yet I think that we both knew instinctively that what we had was a marriage of convenience, a marriage of convention. He had his duties as my husband; I had mine as his wife. There were certain expectations, well-defined roles, but no passion. No spontaneity. Everything had been carefully planned, and artfully executed. What an interesting metaphor that was. I had been the one who had been "executed." Whatever possibilities had existed for my life's fulfillment had been terminated on my wedding day. From then on, it was what Paul wanted, what was best for his career, and therefore for me. That was the focal point of our life together.

It didn't really matter what plans Rita Capri may have had for her own life. All that was laid to rest with the utterance of two little words—"I do." I might just as well have said, "I surrender," since from that moment on, I had become a prisoner to Paul's wishes. My opinions and desires no longer mattered, not even to me.

I don't really know what I had expected marriage to be. It's not as though I had some starry-eyed vision of being rescued from the dungeon by my prince charming. I was much too practical for that. Perhaps too practical for my own good. Not only did I not get a prince who loved me, I also found that my new life was more of a dungeon than my old life had ever been. My home life had been good. My father had been so caring and warm towards my mother and myself, that I came to expect all men to be like him. However, it didn't take many weeks of living with Paul to realize just how uncaring a man could be towards his wife.

As I thought on these things, Beth's words echoed in my mind, and I realized that this was what she had meant by my needing time alone. These were the kind of thoughts I needed to face. How I lived the rest of my life would depend a great deal on what I chose to do in the next few days. These were important moments for Rita. I was planting the seeds of my future in the soil of the here and now. How I viewed my present situation would determine how well I succeeded in this new life.

In the process of dealing with the break-up of my marriage, I could spend my days feeling sorry for myself for having made the mistake of marrying Paul. Or I could realize that I had done what nearly everyone else around me had done. I had made a "good match." Now that I was older, I realized that there's so much more to a relationship that money and social status. There's so much more to being with a man than sharing his bed. Had I realized this before I walked down the bridal path, perhaps I would have tried to find out more about Paul. I might have also realized that while Paul and I might have looked like the perfect wedding cake couple, we were really very different. He wanted to be powerful and successful. I wanted to be loved and nurtured.

I wondered if Paul had been as disappointed with our marriage as I had been. Or had he believed all along that on one side stands his wife, the one who knows how to make him look good; while on the other side hand stands his mistress, the one who knows how to make him feel good? It was disgusting to think about how much power some men hold in their hands. Hands that have been taught how to control, yet seldom how to nurture. Even my father had an element of this nature, however tempered by his religious beliefs. I don't know whether he ever had a mistress, but I know he was cut from pretty much the same cloth as Paul. Paul's view of life was certainly nothing new, and I didn't kid myself by thinking that he would be devastated by losing me. I was every bit as replaceable as my mistress counterpart.

Now that I was choosing another path, I would need to rethink so many things about myself, and my life. Viewing my time alone as solitude rather than loneliness was more than a matter of semantics. It was a matter of control. "Living in solitude" assumed that I was taking control of my life, choosing to be myself. "Living alone" would mean only that my husband and I were getting a divorce. One implied decisive action, the other victimization. One was victory, the other defeat.

I decided to sit down and make a list of things I wanted to do with my life, now that it was my own. I made two headings. One for long-term goals, another for immediate steps I needed to take. Under long-term goals I wrote: "establish a career, become part of the community, travel, and develop a well-defined sense of self." No longer would I be merely someone's daughter or wife. I wanted to become Rita. Just Rita. No more titles that implied someone else's ownership.

I smiled to myself as I realized that Beth was trying her best to keep me from falling into the trap of becoming Rita, Beth's lover. What a wise woman she was. Even though we were close in age, in some ways she seemed centuries older. Did wisdom like hers come from living in solitude? If so, then I wanted to embrace my time alone.

As I pondered my list of goals, I tried to figure out what immediate steps I needed to take in order to move in the direction of fulfillment. I realized that I needed to go job-hunting. I thought about my skills and interests, and realized that what I really wanted to do, was to work in one of the local art galleries. I didn't know the first thing about working in an art gallery, but I had plenty of experience working with people, and some retail experience.

Everything else I could learn.

I had always known that decorating and art were my passions, but I had seldom been allowed to exercise them since I'd been married.   Paul had such strong opinions, and he always knew exactly what he wanted our houses to look like. Our tastes had never been compatible, but I had never shared my opinions with him. He just didn't seem to be interested in hearing about them. I made a note to go and talk to the owners of the galleries in town. That would be step one.

I wasn't sure how to go about becoming part of the community except by talking to people, so I left a question mark next to that goal. I wasn't interested in traveling at the moment. I wanted to put down my roots in Cannon Beach before I began venturing beyond that. I just wrote "later" next to that line. Finally I came to what would be the most important goal of all, that of developing a well-defined sense of self. I made a note to buy myself a diary. Starting immediately, I would begin to record my daily thoughts and activities, in the hopes that it would help me to know myself better.

Feeling sleepy, I decided to go to bed. Then I thought about that big bed in there. I cringed. I didn't want to sleep in that bed. It was Paul's king sized-bed, made for his tall, lanky body. It wasn't Rita's bed. I determined to have Beth help me get rid of it tomorrow. I decided to sleep in one of the other bedrooms for the time being. There were two twin beds in one room, and a queen in the other. I decided to treat myself to the queen-sized bed, as befit a newly coronated queen of the cottage.

I peeled off my clothes, put on an oversized T-shirt and crawled under the covers. The bed seemed very big and empty. I was halfway tempted to switch to one of the twins. But I decided that I would get used to all this space. This was what I had wanted for a long time. I would just have to learn to allow Rita to expand to fill up this space. As my sense of self grew, I felt certain that it would take up more physical and psychological space. I had spent so long trying to fit in the same space as Paul, that I didn't quite know how to relax my grip. Even though I had spent a lot of time alone, while Paul was at work or out of town, I hadn't really felt alone. Knowing that my husband would return soon had somehow kept me from filling all the empty space around me. Now I was free to do that. Take up space. Fill every nook and cranny of my cottage with Rita. With these thoughts occupying my mind, I fell asleep.

When I awoke the next morning, I thought about what had transpired the night before between Beth and I. I thought about her soft flesh, and her quiet passion. I laughed out loud at my memories of Paul grunting like a pig, as he banged away at my body. I wondered how I had ever thought of him as attractive. From the first time we had sex, I had been embarrassed by his sexual side. Out of bed, he was so articulate, so refined. In bed, he was more like an animal in rut.

Sex with Beth had been so beautiful, so poignant. It had made me feel as though I should write a poem about it. But I was no poet, of that much I was certain. I could appreciate beautiful poetry, just as I appreciated art. Yet no beautiful words would flow from my pen, no beautiful paintings from my brush. I was an aficionado of aesthetic beauty, not a creator of it. I would have to be content with that.

As I started to put the coffeepot on, I decided to see if Beth was up, and ready for breakfast. I slipped on my bathrobe and went out to check. I knocked on the door, but there was no answer. I peeked in the window on the side of the camper. I could tell through the crack in the curtain that her bed was empty and neatly made. I hadn't heard her leave, but I had slept pretty soundly. I figured she had gone down to the beach, and I didn't wish to disturb her, so I went back in and fixed breakfast for myself.

After a cup of coffee, a poached egg, and toast with orange marmalade, I got in the shower and rummaged around for something to wear job-hunting. I had to settle for something to wear to go shopping for a job-hunting outfit. Most of my nice clothes were still in Portland. I picked up the telephone, and called the house. I left a message requesting that Paul hire someone to pack my clothes and send them to me. I knew he'd never do it himself, and I wasn't about to leave my sanctuary to go get them. I'd rather do without, than to have to go back there.

I brushed my unruly hair and remembered the hair spray I had thrown away earlier. I retrieved it from the wastebasket, and sprayed my hair into place. I decided to keep it around for such purposes as job-hunting. Then I looked at my face, and decided it was too pale. I scavenged through the trashcan for my discarded foundation, then opted to take out the mascara, blush, and lipstick. By the time I was finished, I had gotten all my cosmetics back out of the trash. I spread them out on the vanity in the master bathroom. I laughed as I realized that wearing makeup was a legitimate part of my personality. I liked how I looked with it. I probably wouldn't put it on just to stay around the house; but it would be nice to have when I faced the public. I quickly put on my face, then went out back to see if I could spot Beth on the beach.

When I didn't find her, I decided to leave a note on her camper door telling her what my plans were for the day. I invited her to eat dinner with me that night. I was anxious to sample her lips again. As I remembered last night, I experienced a surge of sexual energy that started in my chest, and moved down my torso towards my pelvis. I relished this feeling of sensuality, and looked forward to yielding again to Beth's advances. I taped the note on the door, then started walking into town.

I luxuriated in the cool morning breeze that was blowing. I looked out towards the ocean, and fell in love again with the misty mountains that reached out, however tentatively, to touch the sea. I knew I would always love living here. I congratulated myself on my decision to make this my permanent home.

I wandered around downtown searching for a clothing shop that would be able to provide something suitable for job-hunting in Cannon Beach. I wasn't interested in a power suit. I had in mind something more artsy, yet elegant and feminine. I found exactly what I wanted in El Mundo for Women. I bought a black pleated cotton skirt and a silky fuchsia top, with a chain of dancing women embroidered around the chest. It was the kind of thing I had seen some of my more feminist acquaintances wearing. I had wanted something like it for years, but had never dared venture into purchasing clothing that was so unconventional. I had tried on many outfits in the past, but had never actually dared to buy them. I could picture the look Paul would give me if he saw me in something so colorfully bohemian. It just wouldn't have been the thing for the wife of a promising lawyer to wear. Well then, this would be another first for Rita. I wrote them a check from my joint account with Paul.

I went into another shop, and purchased some incense, candles, and candleholders. The candleholders were made of blown glass, done by a local artisan. They were lavender and purple, with long green stems. I also bought a bottle of essential oil, a formula designed to enhance relaxation and clarity of thought. Clear thinking was something I needed badly at the moment.

Next I wandered into the bookstore. I picked out a beautifully bound blank book with marbled inside covers and a burgundy outer cover. I also purchased a book on dealing with divorce.

On my way out the door, I overheard two women talking about the upcoming opening of the latest play at the Coaster Theater. I decided to venture over to them to ask them about it. I loved the theater, especially small community theaters. I thoroughly enjoyed their ingenious ability to improvise with stage sets and costuming. I wondered if they were in need of any volunteers. I stood nearby the two women who were talking, until I finally caught the eye of the taller one. She was very friendly and chatty. I soon found myself drawn into the conversation as though I were a long-time acquaintance.

They were both certain that the theater would embrace a new volunteer with open arms. They encouraged me to talk to the production manager. I was given a name and telephone number to contact. As I started to leave, the woman who had dominated most of the conversation extended her hand to me.

"I'm Emily Thompson, and this is Jade DuBois."

I shook both of their hands, and said, "I'm Rita Capri," surprising myself by using my maiden name. I had the sense that I had wiped out fifteen years of marriage nearly overnight. It felt odd, yet very right. I had lost fifteen years to Paul, but they were fifteen years of nothingness.

Jade excused herself, while Emily went right on talking as though she didn't wish me to leave yet. She paused to give Jade a hug and a peck on the cheek, then bade her good-bye. She turned back to me, and said, "Would you care to get a latte or a cup of tea? There's a nice café near here. I'd like to find out all about our latest Cannon Beach acquisition. This is a delightful little community. Those of us who live here year around are quite chummy."

"I'd love to get something to drink right now. I'm positively parched from all this shopping."

"Thirsty work, isn't it?"

We strolled out the door, and headed for the café. After we had settled ourselves at a table by the window, Emily said, "Do tell me what brings you to Cannon Beach, Rita."

As we drank our beverages, I poured out my story of recently found independence to her. I neglected to tell her about my encounters with Beth. I wasn't sure how this woman would take my lesbian relationship, and I wasn't sure that Beth would want to be a topic of conversation with a stranger.

The more I talked about myself, the more I realized that I already had a self. She had just been shoved into the background when I was with Paul. I found that I could clearly recall my younger, pre-Paul days with crystal clarity, while the time spent with him grew fuzzier by the moment. I finally had to admit to myself that I must've been sleepwalking the entire time I'd been married to him. It was as though I had slipped into a time warp when I had whispered the words "I do." The moment I decided to say, "Oh no I don't," time had returned to normal.

I felt giddy with my newly gained sense of self. My new acquaintance looked at me quizzically. "Are you all right, Rita?"

"Yes. I just had a wave of happiness wash over me."

"That's great. I think I know a little bit about how you feel. I had a relationship of many years that ended two years ago. I recall how freeing it had been, after the first stages of grief had passed, at any rate."

"Well, that's the odd thing. I'm not spending much time and energy on grieving, and it isn't because I'm avoiding it. Maybe it's because the marriage died long ago, and I've only recently realized that it's time to bury the stinking corpse."

We talked for about an hour, then I realized that I should probably go home, put on my new outfit, then head out again. Emily gave me her phone number, and assured me that she was a willing ear, or a shoulder to cry on, whichever I should find myself needing the most. I bade her good-bye, then headed towards home. I saw Jade out of the corner of my eye, as I passed by the bookstore. I was curious as to why she was still there, so I stopped in on the pretense that I had forgotten to buy something. She was talking to a man in casual business attire. He looked a little old to be her husband, but stranger matches have been made. His hair was graying at the temples, and there was an additional sprinkling of gray on top.

When Jade saw me, she enthusiastically waved me over. "Rita, this is Jared, the production manager for the Coaster Theater. I was just telling him about you."

I shook his hand and smiled at him. His blues eyes surveyed my face and figure rather boldly. I was a little uncomfortable under his scrutinizing gaze.

"Jade was just telling me that you share my love of theater."

I nodded.

"Does that love include acting, by any chance?"

I looked at him and frowned. "Well, . . ."

"Come now, no high school or college productions?"

"To tell you truth, yes, but it's been a very long time."

"Rita, excuse me for saying so, but you're not old enough for it to have been a very long time."

Jade excused herself, then went around the counter to ring up a purchase. Until that moment, I hadn't realized that she worked at the bookstore. That definitely explained why she was still hanging around here. I felt a bit awkward with this man who stood before me. I wasn't sure what to say. I hadn't acted since high school. I hardly considered myself an actress. I had just wanted to work with the sets and costumes, anything just to have a reason to hang around and get to know some people in the community.

"It was in high school. I played a small part in a class production of *Our Town*.

"You're kidding me. What a marvelous coincidence! I directed that play when I was in Chicago. And did you enjoy yourself?"

"Yes, I did. Very much."

"Then tell me you'll let me cast you in my next production. I have the perfect role for you. Say you'll consider it. You have three weeks to make a final decision. I'll even throw in a pair of tickets to see our latest play if you'll just tell me you'll consider it."

Feeling slightly overwhelmed, and more that a little pleased at being issued such a flattering invitation, I agreed to consider it. He reached into his jacket pocket and produced two tickets for the Friday evening performance. He pressed them into my hand, allowing his hands to linger on mine much longer than was comfortable for me.

"Excellent. I'll see you there."

Chapter Twelve

I reviewed the day's events as I walked briskly home. I felt a little high from the excitement of meeting new people. It seemed to me that I was on my way towards finding my little niche in the community. As I neared the house, I could see through the window that Beth was inside the camper playing her guitar. I rapped on the door. She opened the door, guitar in hand, and motioned for me come in.

Her eyes smiled at me, as I entered. "You look terribly happy. What have you been up to this morning?"

"I've been in town meeting new people." I related everything that had happened that morning. She sat there listening intently and thoughtfully.

"Sounds like you're doing great, so far. I'm really happy for you, Rita."

"Thank you, yes, I am feeling very good about myself at the moment. Did you get my note about dinner?"

"I did, and I accept. Are we dining in?"

"Whichever you would prefer."

"I'm flexible, and it was your invitation."

"All right then, in it is, though I will probably have to go to the grocery store. Got any ideas?"

"No, but I have some cookbooks we can look at."

"Good, because that's something I don't have here. Paul and I either ate out when we were here, or we'd fix something simple."

"Simple is fine with me."

"Me too. But simple what?"

She pulled two cookbooks out of a drawer in the kitchen, then sat down beside me to look through them. We finally decided on a stuffed bell peppers recipe we found in her *Laurel's Kitchen* cookbook. She made a list of ingredients we would need, then I went back to the house to see what I already had on hand. When I returned to the camper with a shopping list, I noticed that she had put a red plaid flannel shirt over her black T-shirt.

"Are you ready then?"

She smiled, and said, "As I'll ever be. I hope I'm not dressed too formally." She locked the door on the camper, and we started walking towards town.

"You're just right. A true Pacific Northwest

lumberjill."

"You know, in the southeast, if I were to dress like this, everyone would assume that I'm lesbian. Out here, nearly everyone wears denim and flannel. It's hard for me to tell sometimes who's lesbian, and who isn't."

"You mean there's no secret handshake? Now you tell me." I threw up my hands in disgust.

Beth laughed at my antics. "You know, when I was in Seattle this past summer, I concluded that the only dead giveaways there were the ones with nose rings, crewcuts, tattoos, and black army boots. All the others just blend in with the rest of the populace. You pretty much have to hang out at the bars and clubs to be sure you're picking up the right sort of woman."

"Is that something you do often, pick up women in bars?"

"No, that's something I never do. I sometimes go to the bars just to check out the local scene a little, but I've never picked anyone up in a bar. I picked someone up in a bookstore once, but that's another atmosphere altogether."

"Who was she?"

"The women in the bookstore, you mean?"

"Yes."

Beth was quiet for a moment, seemingly lost in thought. Then she said, "Cheryl was her name. She was quite the new age type. I met her in a metaphysical bookstore in Boston. We both reached out and tried to take the same book off the shelf."

"What book was it?"

She shook her head and frowned. "You know, I don't even remember now. We started laughing, and did that polite 'go ahead, you first' thing. In the end, neither one of us even looked at the book. We started talking about books and music, and couldn't stop. It was very funny, but it was definitely one of those times you had to be there in order to appreciate the humor of it."

"And did you sleep with her?"

"For three years."

I stopped walking, turned towards Beth, and put my

hands on my hips. "Three years?   That's not a pick-up, that's a relationship."

She smiled at me, then cleared her throat.   We resumed our walk.

"So what happened to Cheryl?"

"She met a Harvard graduate with a Porsche, and decided she preferred his money to my music."

"Oh. How long ago was that?"

"Eons ago. I was in college."

"Do you still love her?"

"I still love every woman I've made love to. I don't make love without feeling it, and I never stop feeling it once it's over. I just let go and move on."

"What if the other woman doesn't want to let go? Then what?"

"That depends. If it's a good relationship, then it could go on forever, I suppose.   But if it's a bad relationship, I'd have to let go anyway, and leave her to find her own way out."

"Sometimes you really scare me, Beth. I want to know I have something to hang onto with us, yet I feel as though I'm trying to embrace a butterfly. I don't know how to make you stay with me without destroying you. But I do want you to stay. I want to have the chance to get to know you better."

She stared intently at me, frowning. "Do you? How do you know that for sure?"

"I just do. Call it a hunch."

She looked off into the distance. "Hunches are for gamblers, Rita. I'm not a gambler."

"But you'll never find a sure bet."

"Perhaps not."   She paused for a moment, and looked at me. My heart flipped inside. I felt desire clawing at the pit of my stomach, yet somehow it didn't seem like the time and place to act on it. As we headed on towards Osbourn's grocery store, Beth remarked, "Well, that conversation ended on a somber note."

I nodded, trying to swallow my desire for her. I tried to shift my focus outward. I breathed in the afternoon air, and felt the warmth of the sun on my face. I took Beth's hand, as we walked through town. Letting her hand go as I opened the door, I noticed that Emily was heading towards us, apparently on her way out. She looked at me, then at Beth behind me and then back at me.

"Rita! It's nice to see you again so soon. It's certainly a small town, isn't it? Who's your friend here? Another would-be divorcee?"

"This is my . . . friend . . . Beth. Beth, this is Emily, one of the women I met today at the bookstore."

Beth stepped forward, extending her hand towards Emily. They quickly shook hands, then separated abruptly as though repelled by forces unseen. Beth nodded at Emily, and mumbled, "Nice to meet you. Now if you'll excuse me." She quickly walked away, and headed towards the back of the store. Emily and I both followed her retreating figure with our eyes.

Emily spoke first. "Is she new in town too?"

I hesitated, not sure how much I should say about Beth. "I'm not sure. She may just be passing through."

Emily nodded her head slowly, clearly scrutinizing the situation. "I see."

I cringed when she used those two words. I wondered if she had just summed up my whole life, and stuck a label on my forehead. My guess was that it would read, "woman who left her husband to have an affair with a lesbian." I found myself saying, "I'd really like to chat, Emily, but I've got plans for this evening. It was great seeing you again."

"You too, Rita." I followed her distracted gaze, and realized she was still looking at Beth. I felt a pang of jealousy when I realized that Emily was checking out Beth's rear end. As I walked over to join my lover, I mentally replayed my earlier conversation with Emily, trying to remember if she had ever put a gender on that broken relationship she'd mentioned. I couldn't recall it, if she had.

"What are you studying over here?"

She glanced over her shoulder at me. "I'm reading

the ingredients on these cans."

"Is it good reading?"

"No, it's rather boring actually, but infinitely easier than being cruised by your new friend. You do realize that's she lesbian, don't you?"

"Now how do you know that?"

"It's her energy. I can feel it. I take it she doesn't know about me?"

"No, I didn't think it was any of her business. I just met her."

"I thought not. She was clearly surprised to see you with me."

"You're saying that she figured out you're lesbian just by looking at you?"

"Less by looking than by sensing."

"Why do I miss all this unspoken communication?"

"You'll catch on, don't worry. It's just something you get used to. Lesbian body language is a little different from heterosexual body language. It's something you learn by being exposed to it."

"I feel like a babe in the woods."

She looked at me, smiled, and then shook her head.

"Did I say something funny?"

"More like something cute."

"About being a babe in the woods?"

She nodded.

"What's cute about it? Am I missing something again?"

She smiled an even broader smile. "I love your naiveté. It's refreshing."

"I don't know if that's a compliment or not."

"Let's just say that it's really fun for me to be around someone who doesn't speak the language. I'm getting a kick out of translating for you. It makes me aware of how much goes on beneath the surface of a conversation. All the body language—the stares across a crowded room, the posturing. You may think men can be possessive, but trust me, there are lesbians who do everything short of lifting their leg and peeing on their partners when they feel threatened by another woman. It's all terrible amusing. It's the reason I sometimes go to lesbian bars. Every town is a little different, but the language is the same."

"Well, good. At least I have just one new language to learn. I hope you'll start tutoring me soon."

"I am tutoring you, but if you like, we can go to Portland sometime and get some more intensive training."

"Thanks, but I'd like to stay out of Portland for awhile."

"Of course. But from the looks of this town, we may have plenty of local action to check out. It's easier though to observe others quietly, if no one knows you."

We picked up the groceries we needed, then headed back to my house. I caught a glimpse of Emily down by the ice cream shop. I suspected that she had been watching for us from across the street. She turned her back as soon as we came out. We headed back towards home. While we walked, I got my compact out of my purse, and positioned it so I could see down the street behind us. Emily had turned back, and was staring at us.

"Are you doing what I think you're doing with that mirror?"

"Well, if you think I'm watching Emily as she spies on us, then yes I am."

"Let me see that." Beth took the mirror from my hand, and angled it for a view of our voyeur. "By Goddess, she is watching us. I'll have to get me one of those things."

"A compact?"

"Is that what it is?"

"Yes, it has powder on this side, and a mirror . . . well, you saw the mirror."

"It almost looks like a compass I used to have."

I put my compact back in my purse. "I suppose I don't make a very good lesbian."

Beth knitted her brows, and asked, "What makes you say that?"

"Well, I decided today that I want to keep wearing makeup. I like the way it looks on me."

"Yeah, so? You think lesbians don't wear makeup?"

"You don't."

"No, but I'm not the sum total of lesbianism. Your buddy Emily wears makeup, I noticed."

"Yes, she does, but we don't know for certain she's lesbian."

She snorted. "Perhaps you don't know she's lesbian, but there's no doubt in my mind. I know what it feels like to have someone's eyes burning a hole in the seat of my pants."

By that time, we had made it back to the house. We took the groceries in, and put them away. Then we sat down on the couch to rest before beginning dinner preparations. I leaned over and put my head on Beth's shoulder. She put her arm around me.

"I have a confession to make, Beth."

"So soon?"

I nodded. "I was jealous when I saw Emily brazenly staring at your bottom."

"Don't be. It doesn't matter what she does with her eyes."

"It just seemed so obvious."

She laughed. "Yeah, it did, didn't it? She definitely loses points in the subtlety category."

I untucked Beth's T-shirt, and slid my hand underneath it. Her stomach was warm to the touch.

"Is your body always like a heater?"

"Yeah, it makes for a very hot time in the summer."

I wrapped my hand around her breast, and just held it there. I liked feeling its softness, and Beth didn't seem to mind my touching her. I nearly fell asleep like that, resting on Beth's shoulder. Something about her presence seemed to soothe me. As I sat there, leaning against her, I felt safe and secure. There was no need to talk, no need to move. There was no need to do anything except enjoy the moment.

Chapter Thirteen

We sat there for ten minutes or more, not speaking, our breathing synchronized. Finally I stood up, then went into the kitchen to start dinner. Beth followed me. She came up behind me and touched me lightly on the shoulder.

"Thank you for that moment, Rita."

I turned around to look at her, puzzled by this remark. "I don't understand."

"So many people I've met over the years find it impossible to be quiet. They seem to feel that if they can fill the room with sound, then everything will be okay. I don't know whether it's because the silence makes them realize their lives are empty, or what. But it was really nice just to sit there quietly with you, without having sex, without talking. Just existing together."

She paused for a moment and smile at me. "Did you happen to notice that our hearts were beating in unison?"

"I did notice, and I understand what you mean. After you left last night, I suddenly felt very alone. Then I realized that even though I was by myself, I didn't feel lonely. I was experiencing solitude. And do you know what? It felt good. I liked the quiet of the house. I was glad not to have the television blaring. Paul was good at using electronic devices to build walls between us. If I wanted to talk, he would say something like, 'Can it wait until after this show? This is really good, and I'd hate to miss it.' So instead he missed out on me."

Beth wrapped her arms around me from behind. "The man's a fool, Rita. I hope you know that."

"I don't really care what he is. I'm just glad to be rid of him and his noise. I enjoyed that quiet moment with you. It was very peaceful and satisfying for me too."

She kissed me tenderly on my cheek. "What can I do to help you?"

"Nothing. I think I'd like to do this by myself, if you don't mind. You can set the table, then go and wait for me."

"What about that bed frame? Shall I go demolish it for you?"

"I'd like to sell it, so perhaps disassembling it would

be better."

"That's what I meant." She grinned at me, then kissed me playfully on the lips.

I looked at her in mock sternness, "Make sure you get the right bed. I'm sleeping in the queen size one. Please don't tear that one apart."

She laughed and said, "Yes, ma'am. Shall I move it into the master bedroom?"

"That would be very sweet of you, if it's not too much trouble. I want to get a futon, but I don't know how long it will be before that happens. I have lots of things to do with my time, so it may be awhile before it happens."

"I'll take care of it then."

I released myself from her embrace and headed for the utility room. I handed her a hammer from the toolbox, then sent her on her way with a peck on the nose. I could hear her pounding away in the master bedroom, while I banged around in the kitchen fixing dinner. The noise was startling in its contrast from the quiet moments we had just spent with one another. When I was finished with my dinner preparations, I spread everything out on the table, then went in search of my one-woman demolition crew.

"Any hungry women in here?" I looked at the stack of wood piled against the wall. "Wow! I can't believe you've taken both beds apart all ready, and have gotten the queen put together in here. You do quick work."

"I'm not quite finished, but if you'll hold this foot board steady, I'll make sure the rails are tight."

I balanced the foot board while she put the finishing touches on the frame. "I really appreciate your doing this. I don't think I could've done it by myself. Some of those pieces are pretty heavy."

"They are, but one of the jobs I do when I need money is carpentry. Builds the muscles like few other occupations."

"I can imagine. You're an amazing woman, Beth. You do everything from songwriting and singing to construction. A woman of many talents."

"I get around." After one final blow with the

hammer, she said, "There that should do it. You could keep this frame, if you wanted to, and just put a futon mattress on top of the box springs. This is a really sturdy oak frame. It should last a lifetime."

We started putting the sheets back on the bed as we talked. "I do like this bed. I'll have to think about that. It would certainly save me a lot of money. Of course, right now, it's Paul's money."

Beth shook her head at me. "No, don't think that for a moment. That money belongs to both of you. You worked for him without charge for fifteen years. You don't have to wind up a pauper in exchange for your freedom."

"I know, but I hate depending on him."

"You're not depending on him by making him give you what is rightfully yours. Get whatever you need and want from him. You've got only one chance to do it. Don't wind up sorry later."

"All I really want is this house, free and clear."

"Then make sure it's clearly defined in the legal documents that free and clear includes your property taxes. Make him pay them, if you're going to give up the other house totally."

"I hadn't thought about the taxes. You're right about that."

"Do you have a lawyer?"

"Of course. He just happens to work for my husband."

"I kind of figured that. You should probably pick one out here locally, and get to work figuring out how much he's worth. Then make sure you get your due."

"I can see I'm going to need to make another list. I made one last night for life goals and immediate steps to take to attain those goals. I think I need to make another one for things I need to do to get squared away in the next few weeks."

Beth put her hands on her hips, and looked at me with a concerned expression of her face. "Do you really think Paul's going to let you have a divorce without a fight?"

"I don't know. I hope so. I think his guilt over Maddie will work to my advantage. It's bad enough that his wife is divorcing him. If his firm finds out it's because he's been sleeping with one of their secretaries, well, let's just say that they won't be pleased with him. I think he'll be a good boy."

"Well, don't count on it, Rita. People do weird things, unexpected things, in the throes of a break-up. Have you even heard from him yet?"

"No. I called and left a message on the answering machine, but he's technically still on vacation, so he's probably shacked up with Maddie somewhere. I don't know when he'll get the message." We finished making the bed, then returned to the kitchen. "We need to hurry up and eat before our food gets cold."

As we dined on our stuffed bell peppers, we chatted about the possibility of my acting in the local playhouse. Beth seemed to think I would make a good actress. I wasn't so confident of my acting skills.

"Oh come on, Rita. You have quite a lot of passion. I know from first hand experience just how persuasive you can be. Turn that power on when you're up there on the stage, and you'll have them eating out of your hand."

"I appreciate your faith in me. If I had half as much of it, I would feel as though I could do anything."

"You can do anything, Rita. There are no limits. The future will be what you make of it."

"Yes, I realized that last night, as I was puttering around the house. It's kind of scary, to tell you the truth."

After dinner, I put on one of Beth's tapes to copy it. I could tell that it wasn't a professional job, but it didn't really matter. The quality of her voice and her playing came through loud and clear. She was very talented, and I wished she would receive her due for it. When the tape was finished, I handed back the original, and put the copy in my tape carousel.

"Thank you for letting me make a copy of this. I can listen to it at night before I go to bed."

She took the tape from me, then brought my hand

to her lips, lightly kissing it. She looked at me with passion in her eyes. "We could both listen to it tonight, if you'd like."

My heart flip-flopped in my chest. "Does that mean you might spend the night?"

"I could be persuaded, I think. If the right woman were to ask me." She kissed my hand again, then entwined her fingers with mine.

I felt absolutely breathless with desire. "I didn't think you were ever going to stay with me."

"Well, I'm not moving in or anything. But one night shouldn't ruin your development as an individuated woman." She grinned seductively.

"Probably not."

I wrapped my arms around her neck and kissed her deeply. Then I took her hand, and led her to my bedroom. One by one, I undid the buttons on her flannel shirt. Then I pulled off her T-shirt. She eased my shirt over my head, careful not to muss my hair. Then she unsnapped my bra with one hand, and slid it down my arms. I pulled off my slacks and panties, keeping an eye on her as she did the same.

I pulled down the covers, and slid my naked body underneath them. Beth crawled in too, and then reached over to me. In the midst of this activity, I suddenly remembered the incense I had bought at the store today, so I got out of bed and went to get a stick. I brought it back with me, already lit, it's fragrance filling the hallway behind me. I stuck it into an earring holder I had on the vanity, and positioned it so the ashes would fall into the sink.

"I guess I should've bought an incense burner while I was at it. I didn't think of it at the time. I bought this on a whim."

Beth inhaled deeply, while her eyes wander slowly over my body. "It smells great. What is it?"

"Jasmine, I think. I bought several different scents, and I'm not sure which one is which now."

I got back into bed. The aroma of the incense was a satisfying complement to the fragrance of our lovemaking.

I decided that I liked making love to this woman in my bed. I liked her being here, and I hoped she would come to like it enough to stay awhile.

The next morning we got up and had breakfast together. We took turns taking showers, then went for a walk along the beach. I took my camera with me and shot lots of photos of the beach with its gray sand and misty morning fog. Ecola Park was virtually invisible from the beach, so thick was the mist on the mountains. While I paused to change the film in the camera, Beth combed the beach for marine treasures. She picked up an artfully shaped piece of driftwood, and stood there stroking it. When we moved on, she continued to stroke the little piece of wood lovingly.

"It's so smooth," was all she said in the span of a half-hour. I began to wonder if she were meditating, using the wood as a meditative focus device. I walked along in silence beside her, respecting her need to be still inside. Just below the house she stopped and said, "This driftwood has a story to tell. As I walked along rubbing it, I could sense that there was a story inside it."

I looked at her, marveling at this woman beside me who understood the language of the physical world around her. A language I had only begun to know existed. I had begun, only the night before, listening to the whispering of the trees, and the song of the ocean waves. "What kind of story?"

She continued petting the wood, waiting another minute before answering. "A novel or an autobiography. I'm not sure which. I wonder if someone else used to sit and touch it this way while telling it a story. It sounds strange, I know, but I felt as though it were communicating with me, telling me someone else's story." She stopped and looked at me with an expression on her face that revealed a level of vulnerability I didn't know she possessed. "I guess you think I'm odd."

I put my arm around her waist and squeezed her. "I find you unique, Beth, but not odd. I'm not sure I understand exactly about the wood, but I am beginning to understand you a little. You're so creative; you can find a story in every happening in your life. It's who you are. A storyteller with a guitar. A modern day troubadour. I find that fascinating."

"That's a relief. I didn't want you to call the psycho ward on me." She turned away suddenly as though she were about to run away. "I'm not going back there! I'm not, I tell you!" Her eyes flashed at me.

I looked at her defiant, smiling face, and realized that she was pulling my leg. All I said was, "Well, not just yet, but you watch yourself."

We both laughed. Then Beth said, "Do you mind if I go and commune with my newly found friend for awhile? I feel a song coming on, and it helps if I can be by myself."

"Of course I don't mind. I have a whole lot of errands to run this morning. I'll see you later today some time. I may be out during lunch, but if you're interested in sharing my table for supper again, I would be pleased."

"How about coming to my place tonight? It's not fair for you to have to do all the hosting. I know you have a bigger place, but I do have most of the creature comforts."

"It's a date. See you then."

She kissed me lightly before she ran up the stairs towards the camper. I walked along the beach a little farther, wondering how long it would be before my driftwood floated back out to sea. I cherished the moments we had together, but I didn't dare hope it would turn into a permanent arrangement.

I went back to the cottage, and put on my new outfit. I applied my makeup carefully, not wanting to overdo it. A light touch seemed about right for this town. I pulled the mirror out of the closet so I could take in my overall appearance. When I was satisfied that I looked presentable, I walked down Hemlock Street, and began going into each of the galleries along the way. There were two that were my favorites—Haystack Gallery, where I had purchased my Steve Hanks' paintings, and the Bronze Coast Gallery. At Haystack Gallery, the woman who sold me the Hanks' prints recognized me as I came in. We began chatting amiably. I discovered in our conversation that she was co-owner of the place. When I told her I was interested in working at an art gallery, her face lit up.

"Are you really? Well, you know, we don't have any openings right now, but I was just talking to my friend Stacey. She and her husband just opened a new shop up the road a bit. She was saying that she needed to hire a part-time person. If you're interested, I will tell her about you. Would you like that, Mrs. . . . .?"

"Capri. Rita Capri, and I'm divorced, or in the process of getting one, to be precise."

At that moment a woman walked into the gallery. The saleswoman I had been speaking with turned towards her and said, "Ah, Stacey, how fortuitous. I was just talking about you. This woman would like to work in an art gallery. She has very good taste in art. She wiped us out of Steve Hanks' prints earlier this week."

She turned back to me and said, "Rita, this is my good friend Stacey."

I shook hands with Stacey, and we talked for awhile about her art gallery. We really hit it off, and I was pleased when she finally said, "It was so nice to meet you, Rita. Do give me your phone number. I'll give you my card. We'll call you for an interview. My husband, Frederick, is out of town just now, and won't be back for several days. I hope you will still be available."

"Oh yes, definitely. I'm not in a terrible hurry. I would like the job for the joy of working with beautiful objects. I'm not desperate for money."

"Good, we'll talk later then."

I bid them both a good day, then headed for the Bronze Coast Gallery. Every time I made a trip to Cannon Beach in the past, I had always made a point of dropping by this amazing gallery. One glance around the showroom was all it had taken to let me know that the owner had a gift for discovering extremely talented artists.

One piece I found particularly captivating was a large sculpture by Jerry Joslin called "Glory to the Deep." It was a mermaid swimming upside down, with one arm poised by her side, and the other reaching down towards a pearl hiding inside a shell. The twists and bends in the mermaid's body were so artfully executed that you could almost feel the movement of her tail and the stretching of her stomach muscles, as she reached towards the treasure. Her body was so beautiful I longed to reach out and touch her. I stood there for several minutes, mesmerized by this work of art. A woman who worked there, came over and began talking to me about the various artists represented in the gallery. She gave me some brochures on the artists I had been particularly smitten by on this visit. I thanked her warmly for taking so much time with me, then headed out the door in search of food. I had gotten rather hungry from walking around town.

After a quick snack at the Coffee Cabana, I headed up the street towards home. I noticed that Jared was in the bookstore across the street talking to Jade. Or at least they were standing near one another. Jared was talking, but Jade kept looking down at her feet, as though she were either studying something on the floor, or purposefully averting her eyes away from the man beside her. I began to wonder what might be going on between those two.

I decided to go over to the bookstore for the sheer fun of running into someone whose name I already knew. I liked recognizing people as I walked around my new hometown. When I entered the bookstore, Jade was putting books on a shelf. Jared had moved away from her, and was examining some books in the back of the store.

"Good afternoon, Jade."

"Oh hi, Rita. Boy, you must be quite the reader to back in here again."

I smiled, and thought to myself, *Or quite the social butterfly.* Aloud I said, "I go in spurts. Buy a bunch of books, then disappear for awhile. I'm in my buying stage right now, I think. I'm trying to find something good to help me deal with my divorce. The one I bought yesterday looked good, but I skimmed through it a bit, and it seemed as though I should be experiencing all this grief, and to be honest, I'm just not. I'm relieved to get away from my old life."

"Maybe that's a good sign. You know, like you did the right thing, and all."

Jared walked up just then. He was staring at me intensely. "Did I hear you say you're getting a divorce?"

I nodded slowly, puzzled by his interest.

He shifted his weight to one side, and stuffed his hands in the pockets of his white dress slacks. "Funny, I didn't have you picked out as the marrying kind, but I see now that you are wearing a wedding ring." He nodded towards my hand.

I looked down at my hand, startled to see my wedding and engagement ring set staring me in the face. "Oh my God! I forgot all about those. Thank you for mentioning it. It's been only three days now. I was married for fifteen years. These rings feel as though they're part of my hand."

"Perhaps you're not as ready to get divorced as you think." Jared smiled a tight-lipped smile at me. His eyes were completely unreadable.

"Oh no, I'm ready all right." I slipped my rings off my finger and put them in my coin purse to be dealt with later. "I've never been so ready for anything in all my life."

He reached out his well-manicured right hand, taking mine in his. "Well, congratulations then, Rita. If I can do anything for you, or if you need someone to talk to, you just let me know." He patted my captured hand with his own, and looked directly into my eyes.

I glanced at Jade out of the corner of my eye. She was looking at me as though she would like to rip my throat out. Putting two and two together, I figured she must be completely infatuated with him, while he was totally oblivious to her homage. I found that very sad. Jade seemed like such a nice woman, though rather young for a man Jared's age. I hated to see her so smitten with someone who was not the least bit sensitive to her feelings.

I pulled my hand away from Jared's, and adopted a somewhat icy, yet diplomatic tone. "Thank you, but I have someone who is providing me with all the solace I need." I hoped he comprehended the meaning of my words. By the expression on his face, it looked as though he had gotten the message.

He frowned. "Not Emily, I hope."

"What's that?" I asked.

"This person who is consoling you. It isn't Emily Thompson, is it? If so, I'm afraid you might find that her intentions may not be completely honorable."

His patronizing look of concerned annoyed me. I glared back at him. "No, not Emily, though she seems to be a genuinely caring individual.

He took a step back away from me. "Oh, she's caring enough. Too much perhaps."

I wanted to slap the sneer right off his too handsome face. But I restrained myself, saying instead, "Well, I guess I'd better go. I have a few errands to run in town. Good-bye, you two." I gave them a small, friendly wave, then turned away. Jade's cheeks colored at my reference to her and Jared as "you two." She smiled at me, and removed the daggers from my back as I exited the store.

"That was certainly intense," I said to myself as I walked into a nearby shop in the hopes of looking as though I really had something else to do. I had needed to escape from Jared's innuendoes before I told him what I thought of his condescending attitude towards Emily. Besides, my head was beginning to hurt from the effort of reading between his lines.

I browsed through several stores, then made my way back to the bookstore. I didn't see Jared anywhere, so I thought it might be safe to venture in again. Jade was nowhere to be seen either. I went to the self-help section to see if I could find anything that would prove more helpful than the book I had already purchased. I skimmed through several other books on divorce. None of them appealed to me, so I wandered over to the women's studies section. I wasn't sure what I was looking for there. I had never really considered myself a staunch feminist, although I thought equality was a good idea. I was also in favor of a woman choosing whether or not she wished to me a mother. While I found the subject of abortion repulsive, I didn't feel as though giving birth was something that should be forced on anyone.

I discovered that the women's studies section included a wide variety of topic—everything from solo sex to spirituality. I picked up a volume that talked about Goddesses within every woman. I thought it might be interesting. Some of my more liberal friends in Portland had spoken to me of the trend in feminist circles towards reclaiming the Goddesses of ancient times. I had found it mildly amusing, not really being interested in religion. I decided that perhaps now was the time to begin exploring the topics the women's movement had been discussing for decades. I felt as though I were hopelessly behind in my personal liberation.

I also found a book on lesbian health. I wondered what difference it made to your health whether you were lesbian or heterosexual. I decided to purchase those two to see what they had to offer. On my way out, Jade emerged from a room in the back of the store.

"Rita! You're back again." She actually looked pleased to see me.

"Yes, well, I got so distracted talking to Jared about my wedding rings and Emily, I forgot to finish looking around for books. Silly of me really."

"Oh I understand. I always get distracted when Jared is around."

"Do you care for him that much, Jade?"

She looked shaken by my direct question.

"I, um, I . . . Does it show that much?" She brushed a stray lock of blonde hair out of her eyes.

I nodded my head reluctantly.

"Do you think he's noticed? I try not to be obvious." She tugged at the stray lock of hair, causing it to fall back across her face. I wondered if she weren't trying to make herself completely invisible. I felt terrible embarrassing her with my blunt observations of what must've been her heart's deepest secret.

I touched her lightly, yet reassuringly, on the shoulder and said conspiratorially, "Oh well, women see things in other women that men are blind to. I think it's safe to say that he hasn't realized how much you care for him." It was an understatement, albeit a tactful one. I didn't wish to cause her any more anguish than I already had.

She said quietly, "Good. I know he's married, but he's separated, and supposed to be getting a divorce soon, from what I've heard."

"No wonder he was so interested when he heard us talking about divorce."

"Yes, that must have been it."

She seemed to console herself with this thought regarding Jared's interest in my affairs. Wishing to move this discussion away from the topic of men, I asked, "Do you work here full-time?"

"Yeah, but I'm trying to get into clothing design. I have always had rather wild tastes in clothing, so I've been making my own clothes since I was in high school."

I looked down at her delightfully Bohemian dress, then looked back at her face. "Don't tell me you made that dress! It's wonderful."

"You really think so?"

"I do think so. Do you ever sell any of your creations?"

"Well, yeah. The El Mundo carries some of my designs."

"That's marvelous! I love that store. You'll have to show me which ones are yours some time. If your outfit is any indication of your talent, then I'll bet I can find something for my wardrobe. I'm looking for some new clothes to fit my newly found lifestyle as an eccentric and exotic beachcomber."

Jade smiled shyly. "I may have just the thing for you."

"Is it at the store?"

"No. It isn't finished yet. But I'll show it to you as soon as I'm done. I have to work all day today but I'm off tomorrow. I was going to finish it then. If you'd like, I can call you when I'm done with it. I think you're about the right size. I was making it to fit me, but I can always make another one."

"That would be great. Maybe I could wear it to the theater Friday evening, and show it off."   She beamed at my excitement over wearing one of her creations. "I think I'm going to have to make up some personal cards. I seem to be giving my phone number out on a regular basis. Is there a print shop here?"

"Near the post office." She pointed down the street in the appropriate direction.

"Good. I'll jot down my number on the back of one of your bookstore's business cards, but I'll bring you one of my own later."

"Great! I'll call you as soon as it's ready for a fitting. Then if you like it, I can make whatever alterations are necessary for that personalized touch."

"I'll be looking forward to your call, Jade. Take care." I gave her a quick hug, then walked out of the bookstore feeling exhilarated. I was as excited about making a new friend, as I was about finding my own clothing designer. I had been admiring Jade's outfits from the start. I was delighted to discover that she designed and made them herself. It seemed that Cannon Beach was a town overflowing with talent and good taste.

I made a quick stop at the print shop to place an order for business cards. Then I headed for home again. I waved at Jade through the window as I passed by the bookstore one last time on my way up the street. Her enthusiastic smile made me feel warm inside. I had found myself a friend. One who wasn't trying to climb in bed with me. I had to admit that I was puzzled by the attention my impending divorce was giving me. I felt as though I were being viewed as fresh meat. I wasn't sure if I liked that feeling.   It was somewhat flattering, but the blatant drooling was a real turn-off. Here I had practically had to beg Beth to take me to bed with her. Little did I know I would have a whole line of people making offers. It was a comical scene to ponder.

Chapter Fourteen

When I got home, there was a note on my front door. It was from Beth. It read, "Dinner at 'Chez Beth' at 7:00 P.M." I smiled, then checked my watch. I had three hours until our dinner date, so I went inside, and settled down to read my books. The book on lesbian health was a quick read. I finished it in a couple hours, then laid it aside to see if Beth would like to read it too. It was pretty general, but I did learn a thing or two about breast cancer and lesbians, as well as about sexually transmitted diseases.

I started to look at the book on Goddesses, but it looked as though it would be more intensive, and I wasn't ready to get started on it yet. Instead I pulled out my journal, and began making notes of my social progress. I found that it helped me to pull my thoughts together. It also helped me to examine my interactions with the people I had encountered. I realized that I would have to watch out for both Jared and Emily, especially if I were going to get involved with the theater. They were both part of that community, and I wasn't sure I wanted to get too close to either of them.

I was just about to change my clothes when the phone rang.

"Hello?"

"Rita, this is Paul. I got your message about the clothes. You're not still serious about getting a divorce, are you? You must understand that Maddie means nothing to me. She's just a little seductress who caught me off guard. There's nothing to it really. Just a midlife fling. You've got to realize that."

I waited patiently for Paul to finish his well-polished speech.

"Are you quite finished? First of all, I am fully aware that Maddie means nothing to you. I'm also aware that I mean nothing to you, except to prove to your firm that you're a stable, successful lawyer, worthy of full partnership in the not-too-distant future. I've been your trophy wife all these years, and it's a job I no longer wish to have. I quit, Paul. I want a life of my own. Friends of my own. A house of my own. I'm not asking you to support me for the rest of my life. I wish only to have my things sent to this house. I want this house, Paul. Nothing else from you. You can keep both cars if you like. I know you love the beemer. Of course, if you don't want the Volvo, I'll take it. It's more practical for my needs anyway."

"I don't give a damn about the stupid Volvo. For God's sake, Rita, I can't believe you're doing this to me! What have I ever done to you?"

"Aside from having affairs, and not loving me?"

"What affairs? Maddie means nothing, I'm telling you."

"Perhaps not, but I'm sure the firm wouldn't appreciate it, if they find out."

"You wouldn't tell them, would you?"

"Only if you hassle me over this divorce. Get used to it, Paul. We never loved each other. We married because it was a good match for us and our families. That's all. I refuse to live such a shallow life any more. I don't know why I put up with it as long as I did. And as for your affairs, I rather suspect that Jill Aikens was the first of your meaningless flings."

There was silence on the other end of the line.

"I knew it, Paul. I knew it then. I just couldn't bring myself to admit it."

"That was years ago, Rita."

"How many were there between Jill and Maddie? Five, ten, twenty?"

"Rita, you don't know what you're saying."

"You want me to start naming other names. Oh, I've known all along, Paul. I just haven't wanted to face the truth. But I'm facing it now, and do you know what? None of those things matters. If we had loved each other the way a married couple is supposed to love each other, then there wouldn't have been room for all those flings. I had nothing to offer you but an appearance of matrimonial happiness. It was a facade. But now the facade has crumbled, and there is nothing left except a rotting building, sitting on a nonexistent foundation."

"It's over, Paul. Don't fight me on this divorce. You may have an entire army of attorneys at your disposal, but I have the truth. How many names would I have to name before the firm dropped you all the way down to basement level? Now send me my things, and don't bother calling me again unless you have something important to say to me. I certainly have nothing else to say to you."

I hung up the phone, shocked at my own audacity. Then I laughed until I cried. After this tidal wave of emotion subsided, I realized that I needed a shower before I went to dinner. I threw off my clothes and got into the tub. I scrubbed myself vigorously with soap, as though I needed to scrub off the very skin I had worn as Paul's wife. I knew that he was not an evil man. I even knew that in different circumstances, he might have made someone a decent husband. But we'd had a loveless marriage far too long. He had coped with it by having affairs with secretaries and, if my suspicions were on the mark, a few of his fellow lawyers' wives. I had coped by going numb.

Now things had changed. He could have all the flesh he could consume without fear of my reprisal. I could reclaim my emotions. I would live life to the fullest, embracing both pleasure and pain to my utmost capacity. And if he didn't like it, he could bloody well go to hell.

I stepped out of the shower feeling invigorated. I toweled myself off, then got dressed quickly. I longed to have access to my complete wardrobe. I was getting weary of the few outfits I had brought with me to the beach for the week. Each article of clothing was a clinging reminder of who I had been. I knew I would have to revamp my entire wardrobe when it arrived. There would be some things I could keep, but most of it would have to go to charity. As I continued to shed the chrysalis of my past, I found that few of my clothes fit the woman I was becoming. I finally settled on a simple outfit of beige knit slacks and a light green summer-weight sweater. I went off to *Chez*

Beth sporting a ravenous appetite for authentic living.

I tapped lightly on the camper door, then opened it since she was expecting me.

"Welcome to Chez Beth."   She bowed towards me. When she straightened up, she took one look at me, then said, "What on earth happened to you?"

"What do you mean by that?"

"That expression on your face. I don't know, it kind of looks like it's announcing to the world, 'Look out, everybody, here comes Rita!'"

I laughed. "I didn't realize it would be so obvious. I had it out again with Paul on the phone. He tried to talk me out of the divorce."

"Oh, to have been a fly on the wall. I can imagine what you said, but I'd like to hear it from your lips."

I leaned against the kitchen cabinets, and folded my arms across my chest. "I was angry, Beth. Really angry. Especially when I started realizing just how many affairs he's had over the years. It just burns me up. Here he was sleeping with every willing woman who crossed his path, while I was walling off my emotions, not allowing myself to experience any of them. No pleasure. No pain. Nothing but an emotional vacuum."

"That's good, Rita. Anger is part of the healing process."

"I know. I may not spend a whole lot of time being sad that the marriage is over, but I have a feeling I haven't seen the last of the anger. The funny thing is that I can't hate Paul any more than I could love him. There's only indifference."

"A wise woman once told me that the opposite of love is not hate, but indifference."

"Well, it certainly describes my attitude towards Paul. I'm not even really angry about all his petty little affairs. That was his way of coping with the emptiness of our life together. What I really regret is that my method of coping was not to cope. Just ignore everything. Don't notice that he comes home late from work every day. Don't notice that he has to take all his calls in his private library.

Don't notice that I never experience sexual desire, or desire of any kind, for that matter. I'm angry with myself for not dealing with the situation. I copped out completely. Totally abdicated the throne of my emotions."

She wrapped her arms around me and held me close to her body. "But at least you realize that now, and have begun to live again."

"Yes, that is the saving grace in this whole ordeal. I have begun to live again. Thank you for being here, Beth. It helps. I know you're probably not going to be around forever, but I'm thankful for the time we have."

I squeezed her tightly, then backed away from her. As I calmed down, I looked around and realized that Beth had decorated the camper with candles and a floral centerpiece.

"Beth, it's lovely. You did a lot of work to make this look like a little restaurant. How sweet. And here I am bursting into your lovely café, shouting and moaning about my divorce. I'm sorry. That was terribly insensitive of me."

She pulled out my chair and motioned for me to be seated. She sat down next to me, and placed her hand over mine. "Don't be sorry. I asked for it. I'm glad you had such a stimulating discussion with Paul. It's good for the soul."

"You're so understanding. So compassionate. How do you do that?"

"Do what?"

"Behave as though you truly care."

"I'm not really sure how to answer that, because I do care. I can't make you heal any faster. I can't give you back the last fifteen years. But I can be here right now, offering my support and encouragement. It's not so much something I do, as it is who I am. Does that make sense?"

"It makes perfect sense. It's just that it's so hard to believe. There are a lot of different types of people in the world, but you're unique. You don't really fit any type of personality I've ever met. You must realize that you are different."

"I guess so. I don't know why it is that way. I only know that it is. Maybe it comes of counting my heartbeats every night. I know there are only so many heartbeats in any given life. I try not to waste any of mine."

"That must be hard work."

"No. That's exactly what it is not. It isn't work. It's simply a matter of being alive in the moment. Living in the here and now. I live each heartbeat as though it were an entire lifetime. I want to make each one count, Rita. I want to make a difference. When you don't waste any of your heartbeats on things that don't matter, then it is easy. I learned the hard way that wasted efforts lead to more difficulties ahead. I don't fret over the things I can't change. I let them be."

"I have no answer for that."

Beth leaned back in her chair and studied my face. "Do you need a comeback for everything?"

"No, it's not that. It's just that the conversation ends there, with naked truth."

"Then let it be. Don't try to dress it up."

I stopped talking, and let her words sink in. To live without wasted heartbeats. How would you go about doing that? By counting your heartbeats at night? But surely there was more to it than that. By being aware of everyone and everything around you? That would be exhausting. Perhaps it required merely being aware of yourself and your own feelings. That was a lesson I desperately needed to learn, I thought to myself. Aloud, I asked, "When you say you listen to your heartbeats, do you mean that in a literal sense?"

"Yes and no."

"Sometimes it is too noisy in this world to hear your heartbeat literally. But because I'm practiced at it, I can at least always sense my heartbeat. I know it's there, and I try to stay focused on it, for the gift of life resides in that place of listening."

"Have you always done this?"

"No. I used to get caught up in the whirling sands of time. Now it's a rare thing if I know what time it is. As you can see, I don't wear a watch. I don't even own one any more. There's a clock in here, but I seldom pay any attention to it."

"So was it your travels that taught you this?"

"Not my travels in themselves. I began traveling because I realized that I could no longer tell whether my heart was beating inside me. During my travels, I regained that sense of my heart. You see, when I was a child, I used to lie in bed, listening to the sounds of the night. I grew up in the countryside of Kentucky, so the sounds I heard were nature's sounds. Croaking frogs and chirping crickets.

"Every once in awhile the night would get very quiet. One time, during one of these moments of sudden stillness, I noticed that there was a rhythmic pounding in my head. I wasn't sure at first what it was, but then I realized that it was my own heart. After that I began to listen for my heart. It was a game at first, but as I grew older it became more of a meditation.

"Then about five years ago, when things started going haywire, I realized that somewhere along the course of my life, I had stopped listening to my heart. It was almost as though it had stopped beating. It scared me, I'll tell you. I thought I had died, and in a sense, I had died, for I was no longer living in harmony with my life's own drumbeat.

"It seems to me that most people spend their whole life trying to avoid listening to their own heart. They are afraid of what they will hear. Will they hear that their life has gotten off track, like mine had? Or will they hear the sounds of their own mortality? The truth your heartbeat speaks is the same truth you find when you look in the mirror. There's only you. That's all you have control over. Yourself, and no one else. This is your chance to look into the mirror of your own heart, Rita. What do you think you'll find?"

Perplexed, I shook my head at her, then asked, "What do you find, Beth?"

"I find Beth. That's all. I'm all there is. You are all there is for you. When all is said and done, all relationships in this dimension of existence are temporal. We can't afford to build our lives around other people. We have to build them around the truth we find in each of our hearts. If we are lucky enough to find someone who can honor that truth, while remaining true to their own inner voice, then we are blessed indeed. And if each of us would learn to listen to our heartbeats, we'd have a lot fewer people hurting themselves and the people around them."

"But what if your truth isn't the same as mine?"

"I believe the same basic truth is in each of our hearts. It has reverberated throughout the millennia, embraced by all the religions of the world, yet not limited to religion because there are those who hold to no religion who say the same thing. Our individual paths may lead us down many different roads, but all roads lead to the same truth."

"And that is?"

"Love, respect, and compassion for all living beings. If you can honor and love all of creation, then you can live in harmony with it. But it starts with learning to love and honor yourself."

I waited for more, but she had stopped talking. I was at a loss for words, so the silence that fell upon us was heavy, yet comforting. I allowed the blanketing silence to remain as long as I could, then said softly, "Well, that was one hell of an appetizer. Where do we go from here?"

She smiled, then got up and began to serve me my dinner. First we had a tossed garden salad. Then we ate the spinach quiche she had made. It was delicious. I ate slowly, savoring each bite. Savoring each moment. Maybe even savoring a few of my heartbeats. After dinner, she told me that she wanted to play her new song for me. I leaned back in the chair, and closed my eyes, so I could allow her music to paint a picture on the canvas of my soul. I felt the words; I felt the music. I was alive with the joy of living, or in keeping with the French theme of the evening, make that *joie de vie.*

When she had finished the song, I asked her to sing it again. This time I picked up the piece of driftwood that had been sitting on the table as part of the centerpiece. I stroked it lovingly, while she sang me the story it had to tell. It wasn't what I had expected, and the words didn't make a lot of sense to my head. Yet somewhere in my heart I found that I understood the message, and that message was meant for me at that moment in time. These are the words she sang:

> Pieces and pieces
> All fit together
> They form a lifetime
> Weighed with the feather
>
> Pieces of poetry
> Pieces of pie
> Floating like driftwood
> Down from the sky
>
> Pieces and pieces
> All so elusive
> Part of the puzzle
> They know what they give
>
> Pieces of poetry
> Pieces of pie
> Floating like driftwood
> Down from the sky
>
> Pieces and pieces
> Words of the sages
> Yielding the same truth
> Throughout the ages
>
> Pieces of poetry
> Pieces of pie
> All fit together
> The day we die

Chapter Fifteen

When she had finished singing, we sat in silence for a few moments. Then I climbed up onto her bed and lay there listening to the quietness. I placed my hand over my heart. I felt its faint drumming against my fingertips. I counted each beat, one by one, until I lost count. Then I began counting again. Finally I broke the silence. "Beth?"

"Yes?"

"What next?"

"What do you mean?"

"Where do I go from here?" I was feeling very small and unsure of myself.

"Where do you want to go, Rita?"

"I want to stay right here. In Cannon Beach. In my house."

She shrugged her shoulders. "Then do so."

"Yes, but what should I do next? Should I go on an extensive job search? Take a class? Get involved with the theater"

She leaned her guitar against the chair she'd been sitting in, and stretched out next to me in the loft bed. She didn't saying anything at first. She just stared up at the ceiling. I thought that she must have forgotten the questions I had asked, or perhaps had figured they were rhetorical. Finally she asked, "Do you want to do those things?"

"Yes, but not just yet."

"What do you want to do then?"

"Nothing. I just want to do nothing. At least not right away."

"Then do nothing."

"That seems so foreign to me. I used to have a full calendar, what with all the causes and charities I used to support. I feel as though I should be doing something with my life."

"What would that something be?"

"I don't know."

She rolled onto her side and laid her head on my shoulder. "Then be quiet and listen until you do know. Listen for your heart wherever you are, whatever you're doing. If your heart becomes too distant to be heard, then you are walking in the wrong direction. Find a way to live close to the sound of your heart. Anything that keeps you from doing that, is something you can live without."

"I see."

"Yes, I do believe you do."

She smiled up at me and gently placed her hand over the hand that lay across my heart.

"I can see you're growing, Rita. You were ready for this metamorphosis. You have completed your time in the cocoon. Now you are emerging from your sleep, a beautiful butterfly."

"I feel like a different person."

"You are a different person. I have heard it said that people do not change. It isn't true. We are all capable of change. When we do not change, we do not grow. When we stop growing, we die. One of my college professors used to say, 'What you feed grows; what you starve dies.' I have found that to be true. If you feed your addictions, they will grow. If you feed your passions, they will grow. You choose what aspects of yourself you will cultivate."

"You make my head hurt with your words."

She sat up, grinning at me. "That's just your brain trying to grow."

I sat up too, and looked out the window of the camper. "Well, it feels as though it's about to explode."

"Perhaps we should lighten up for the time being. Give you some time to absorb everything you are feeling and thinking."

"Perhaps. Would you like to come to the house?"

"No, I think maybe you should spend some time alone. I don't want to crowd your thoughts. Go and listen to your heart, Rita. I will stay here and listen to my mine. It seems to be saying a lot of things to me lately."

I slid down off the bed and turned to face her. "Like what?"

She held her index finger to her lips. "Shh. Not yet. I will tell you later, when I have had more time to think about it."

I nodded. As I started to head for the door, she jumped down from the bed, and grabbed my arm. She turned me around so she could look into my eyes. I thought I saw tears.

"What is it, Beth?"

She shook her head, then released my arm. "No, not yet."

"You're going to leave me, aren't you?"

She was silent for several extremely long seconds. "I think so. You need time alone. I need some time alone too. I'm torn between staying here and cultivating this relationship, and leaving for awhile, so you can cultivate your soul without having to worry about building a relationship with me."

"What does your heart say?"

"It says that my love for you will wait patiently."

"So you will leave?"

"But my head says, 'Yes, but what if she grows beyond her need for your love?'"

I looked at her, shocked by her confession of insecurity. "You're afraid I will not want your love in the future?"

She nodded her head, then bowed it.

"Beth, you do what your heart is telling you to do. I would like it very much if you stayed, and yet I will understand if you need to go. In fact, I think you should go. I've been holding my breath ever since I met you, wondering how long it would be until you drifted away from me. Go now before I come to expect your constancy. If you wish to return, then I will welcome you. I may be a changed person, but I can't imagine that I will be so changed that I will no longer love you."

She wiped a tear from her eyes, then sat down. "I'll think about it. You think I'm just drifting away you, don't you?"

Tears spilled down my cheeks. "I've been expecting

it from the start."

"That's not what this is all about, Rita. I want you to have room to grow without my being a distraction. I need to see if I am willing to come back again. For the first time in a long time, I feel as though I've found a reason to stop moving. But it's a little too complicated right now. If I settle down here in Cannon Beach right now, then you will have had no time to develop your personality on your own. You will go from being Paul's wife to Beth's lover. There needs to be an in-between stage for you. And to be honest, I think I need an in-between stage too. It's not easy to go from being a moorless ship to a docked one. I need some time to evaluate, to make the transition. Do you understand that?"

"I do understand, Beth, and as much as it hurts to say this, I think you're right. I need for you to go away for awhile. But how will we know when it's time for you to come back? Will you stay in contact with me?"

"I don't know. Occasionally perhaps, but not often. Otherwise it will just become a long-distance relationship, still requiring a great deal of care. You need to be on your own, completely. But I think our hearts will know when it's time."

"Yes," I said. "Our hearts will know." I stood there for a moment envisioning myself standing on the dock waving to her, as she hoisted the sails of her ship and headed out to sea.

I walked out the door of the camper, and went inside the house. I made myself a cup of tea, then sat down to stare out at the ocean, straining to see if her ship had already sailed beyond the visible horizon. I wanted to cry, for I knew that losing Beth was going to hurt a hell of a lot more than walking away from fifteen years with Paul. But no tears would come. It wasn't that I was numb; it was that I was in shock. I had expected her not to stay. I hadn't expected to find that she was leaving even though she wanted to be with me. The drifter wanted to stop drifting, to settle down near me. But we both knew I wasn't ready to start a new relationship.

As I sat there staring out the window, I found that I could feel the beating of my heart. I tried hard to hear what it had to say. As I suspected, it said, "Let her go. You will never lose her love." I believed it, even though one part of me wanted to make her stay.

I don't know how long I sat there in silence, listening to my heart as it kept time with the pounding of the waves. When I finally stood up, I discovered that I had gotten stiff in the legs. After I stretched a bit in an attempt to loosen up my muscles, I headed for the kitchen. I washed my teacup, then headed for bed. As soon as my head hit the pillow, my heart burst open wide. I cried myself to sleep.

When I awoke the next morning, I half expected to find the camper gone. But there it stood, as steadfast and stalwart as ever. I got in the shower to see if it could revive my weary heart. I felt hung over. I had a headache from shedding too many tears. As I showered, I wondered how long it would be until she returned. Then I chided myself for getting ahead of the moment. "Live for today," I reminded myself. "She's still here for time being. Enjoy her company; then let her go without clutching your heart. Feel the pain of her departure. Then if she returns to you one day, bask in the rapture of her love."

I stepped out of the shower, and set my mind to the task of picking out something to wear. When I came out of the bathroom, she was standing there with a tray of food in her hands. "I came to serve you breakfast in bed, but I see you're already up."

"Hi. I was just about to get dressed."

"Oh, don't bother. It won't be necessary for what I have in mind."

"No?"

"Definitely not," She said with a sexy smile. Having set the tray on the dresser, Beth walked over to me. She took the towel from my hand, and finished drying me off, kissing me all over, as she went. Taking me by the hand, she led me over to the bed, and pulled back the covers.

"Now pretend you're just waking up again."

I got back into bed. "Oh, please. Do I have to? I woke up with a pounding headache."

Her playful tone turned more serious. "I'm sorry. Does it still hurt?"

"Only a little. The shower helped, I think."

She slid into bed next to me. "Let me massage your scalp. That should wipe it out completely. Just relax in my hands."

She massaged my head, my neck, and my shoulders until not only had my headache gone away, but so had my memory of the pain I had felt the night before. Beth has here now. Everything was all right.

Finally she said, "How's your head?"

I smiled lazily at her. "What head?"

"I take it that's a good sign."

"Yes, I feel wonderful. You do have the most talented hands."

"Thank you. I hire them out on occasion to make a little extra money."

"What's that supposed to mean?"

She laughed under her breath. "Nothing. Just a little joke." She rearranged her body so she could look at me better. I leaned over to kiss her. She shook her head, then said, "Wait. Let me feed you breakfast first. You'll need your strength."

I raised my eyebrows at her. "I think I like the sounds of that."

She got up, and brought the tray over to the bed. She set it on the nightstand, then picked up the bowl of fresh strawberries. She hand fed them to me, dipping them first in whipped cream. I fed some to her too. When we were finished with the fruit, she stuck her finger in the bowl of whipped cream, then began smearing the leftover cream on my body. She covered my nipples, circled my navel, and dotted my rib cage with it. Then she began licking it off. She got some on her face, so I licked it off for her. Then we kissed slowly, passionately, hungrily.

I tried not to wonder if this would be the last time we made love, but I did anyway. Somehow it made that whole act more sacred, more poignant, more precious. I knew I would never love another soul the way I loved Beth. Even if she never returned, she would be the one who had touched my heart forever. How could I have even begun to think that I could embrace this butterfly of a woman? *Let her go!* My heart screamed. *She will be destroyed if you try to hold onto her. Let her decide whether she will alight near you. Set her free!*

As my body convulsed under her touch, I felt inside that it would be all right. I would be able to live without her. When I tried to reciprocate her passion, she shook her head. "Not today. I have my period. It will make me cramp."

I nodded my understanding, and tried not to feel cheated by nature. *Let it be*, my heart said. *Don't worry about the things you cannot change.*

"I love you, Beth."

"I love you, Rita."

Then she got up and took the tray out with her. I put on my bathrobe, and followed her into the kitchen. She began making breakfast.

"What are you doing?"

"I figured you would still be hungry. You didn't eat that much, you know. How would you like your eggs?"

"How about scrambled?"

"Done. Now sit down in your chair, and let me pamper you this morning. I bet you don't remember the last time you were pampered."

"Of course I do. I was ten years old, and I had the chicken pox. My mother stayed with me nearly the whole time, taking care of me."

"That long ago, huh? That's not good. Everyone needs to be pampered sometimes."

"I won't argue with you there."

I sat down in the bentwood rocker, and began reading the book on Goddesses. Within minutes, Beth had set the table, and served up our scrambled eggs, toast, and orange juice.

"It's ready."

"And so am I. I'm hungry. You made me work up an appetite." I smiled coyly at her.

"I aim to please."

"You're a very good shot."

We chatted comfortably over breakfast. It was almost too lighthearted. I got the feeling I wasn't the only who didn't want to broach the subject of her imminent departure. As we were clearing away the breakfast mess, the telephone rang. I walked over and picked up the receiver. "Hello?"

"Hi. Is this Rita?"

"Yes, it is," I said, puzzled, not recognizing the voice on the other end of the line.

"This is Jade, from the bookstore."

"Well, hello, Jade. Surely you're not ready for me already?"

"Yes, I am actually. I got so excited about the dress that I came home last night and finished it. It's ready for a fitting whenever you are."

"Are you at home now?"

"I am."

She gave me her address, and I promised to be there in roughly an hour. Then I hung up. Beth had an interested look on her face when I got off the phone.

"Good news?"

"You might say that. That was Jade, a woman I met at the bookstore. She works there, but she also designs clothing on the side. I'm supposed to go over to her house today to be fitted for a dress she thinks I might like."

"Wow! Your very own clothing designer. Very impressive."

I couldn't tell whether she was being facetious. "I know you don't care about clothes, but I really need a new look. I'm tired of the middle-aged yuppie housewife look. I need something new to express the new me."

"Sounds exciting," She said in an even-keeled tone.

"Yes, well it is for me."

She frowned at me, and cocked her had to one side. "You think I don't approve, don't you?"

"I'm not sure what I think."

She smiled reassuringly at me. "Just because I don't care about fashion, doesn't mean I expect you not to. Beth doesn't care about it. Rita isn't Beth, so she can have her own tastes. Will you come and model it for me when you get back?"

"Sure, if I buy it. I haven't even seen it yet. It was something she had been making for herself."

"Ah, I see. Well, I'd better be going. I'll probably be in and out today, so if I'm not at the camper when you get back, just leave me a note telling me you're home."

"Okay. Have a wonderful day, Beth. Thank you for making the morning so memorable."

"You're quite welcome."

I kissed her cheek before she walked out the door. Then I went to get my purse and my keys. I decided I'd better take the car, since I wasn't sure just how far away Jade's house was.

Chapter Sixteen

I found Jade's house without a problem. I fairly leaped up the stairs to her front door. I was so excited. I rang the doorbell, and surveyed the view of the ocean while I waited. Jade peeked through the curtain that covered the glass on the front door. She saw me and smiled, then opened the door wide.

"Hi, Rita. I'm so glad you're here. I'm really excited. I do hope you like it, but don't say you do if you don't, okay?"

"I promise to give you my honest impression."

"Good. It's back here in the sewing room."

We walked through the living room and dining room, and into what was probably intended to be a breakfast nook. It was a small room that was filled from corner to corner. An industrial sewing machine took up most of the space. The rest of the space was cluttered with sewing baskets and boxes of accessories. Several bolts of cloth leaned against one wall. A sewing dummy stood in one corner, covered by a plastic trash bag.

"Is that it?" I pointed to the dummy. "You're trying to kill me with suspense, aren't you?"

She nodded her head vigorously. Then she reached over and grabbed hold of the bag. "The drum roll please."

I tried to imitate the sound of drumming with my mouth.

"And now for the unveiling of Jade's masterpiece!"

She whipped off the bag with a quick yank. I looked at it. Then I looked at her expectant face. Then I looked at it again. "You made this?" She nodded her head. "My God, young lady, it's incredible! How long have you been sewing?"

"Since I was old enough to hold a needle and thread."

"It's beautiful. You mean to tell me you're actually willing to part with this? It's too beautiful for words. Quick tell me how much I owe you for it. I want to buy it before you come to your senses."

She laughed, and spun around in a circle. "It is beautiful, isn't it? I just knew you were going to love it. It had Rita written all over it."

"Does it really look like me?"

She nodded again, eyes flashing.

"Wow! I've always wanted to have a dress like this, but never had the courage. I was so afraid it would be too exotic for my conservative husband's tastes. But now I don't have to worry about him any more. Really, how much do you want for it?"

She shook her head. "Nothing."

"What? Surely not. I've got money. I'm not broke. How much?"

"No, Rita. I'm serious. It's a gift. If you'd like for me to design more clothes for you, then I will let you pay me for those. But this is a gift from me to you. Consider it a welcoming gift."

"At least let me pay you for your expenses then."

"Nope. You can repay me by wearing it proudly. You can advertise for me." She beamed her excitement and pride.

I examined the dress closely, noting the excellent needlework. "You're a talented woman, Jade. I'm touched by your generosity. I'm going to wear it tomorrow night to the play. That should be a good chance to advertise, yes?"

"Yes!"

I hugged her neck, then hugged the dummy. Then I hugged her again. I got choked up as I thought about how much time this young woman had spent on this work of art. For work of art it was. The skirt was full, and made from finely spun cotton. It was an aqua color. The bodice was coral and aqua, with intricate embroidering on it. It was a stylistic rendering of the marine life found here at Cannon Beach—starfishes and anemones, crabs and seaweed. It was quite good. I was overwhelmed by her gift of beauty.

She took the dress off the dummy and pressed it into my hands. "Now go in my bedroom, and try it on. It's back through the dining room and down the hallway to the end. It's the last room on the right. I'll wait here for you."

I did as I was told. I turned around in front of the mirror in Jade's bedroom, admiring the dress. Then I looked at my own face, and realized that this dress had indeed been made for Rita Capri. It was my dress, my new look. Part Bohemian, part heiress. It was an incredible combination. I walked back to the sewing room. Jade looked carefully at me, then motioned for me to turn around slowly. She armed her mouth with a half dozen straight pins and went to work, pinning and tucking. When she was finished, she took the last pin out of her mouth, and said, "You know, I didn't design this to hang quite this way, and it wouldn't have looked right on me. But I like it better this way on you. See what you think. There's a mirror behind the door there.

I looked in the mirror, not quite sure what she had done. I couldn't quite articulate it, but she had altered it in a way that made it even more flattering. I marveled at

Jade's talent. She was a genius, in her own way. A shy, unassuming, designing genius. I went back to the bedroom to change into my other clothes. When I handed her the dress, she asked, "Got another minute? This won't take long."

She flipped the dress inside out, then stuck it under the sewing machine needle, and went to work. Her hands worked quickly and confidently. In less than ten minutes, she handed it back. "It's done, if you'd like to try it on again."

I started to take the dress back to the bedroom, then said, "Look, if you're going to be making clothes for me, you're just going to have to get used to seeing me in my underwear." She blushed, as I closed the door to the sewing room, and lowered the shade on the one window in the room. She turned her back, while I changed. I smiled at her sense of privacy. "Okay. How do I look?"

She frowned, and squinted, as I turned slowly around. "Well, it looks wonderful to me. What do you think?"

"I looked in the mirror. It's perfect. Absolutely perfect. When can I commission you for the next one?"

She smiled. "Just say the word."

"I'll do that, but I should go now. I don't know how to thank you. Can I at least take you out to dinner some time? What's your favorite restaurant in town?"

"Well, I know it's not a fancy place, but I rather like the Homegrown Café."

"I haven't been there yet, though I've heard it's good. May I treat you to dinner soon?"

She nodded. I hugged her again before I left. I didn't even bother taking the dress off. I wanted to wear it forever. As I drove home, I wondered what Beth would think of it. My heart froze when I got within sight of the house, and saw that the camper was gone. As I pulled into the driveway, I nearly began crying. "Not yet, Beth, not yet!"

There was a note attached to the front door. It read, "I'll be back soon. I need to take the truck for a drive.

It's been parked for too long. See you later."

I tried to assure myself that Beth wouldn't just leave without saying good-bye. I went inside and changed into my other clothes. I had wanted to surprise Beth by coming home in the dress. Since she wasn't home, I decided to hang it up, so it wouldn't wrinkle in the interim.

I decided to call my parents. I hadn't told them about the divorce yet. I had wanted some time to think about everything first. I felt that I was as ready as I'd ever be, so I dialed their number. My mother answered the phone, for which I was thankful. I had wanted to break the news to her first. I explained everything to her, all the years of loneliness and emptiness, as well as Paul's affairs. I asked her not to tell my father about the affairs. I was afraid of what he might do to Paul. My father was a rich and powerful man, and not above making things uncomfortable for his daughter's unfaithful husband.

I didn't tell her about Beth. I didn't think she would understand. It wasn't that I was ashamed of her, or of our love. It's just that I didn't see the point in it, if she were only going to disappear from my life again. If she came back to me, then I would let them know. In the meantime, I didn't want them to think that she was in any way responsible for my choosing so suddenly to leave Paul. At least not in the way they were bound to interpret it.

My mother waited until I was finished, then said, "I'm sorry. I can't say that I'm terribly surprised, but I am sorry. I had hoped you would at least grow to love each other, as your father and I have. I knew you weren't in love with him when you married him. I'm sorry I didn't say anything at the time. I guess I hoped it would right itself over the years, but I see now that it didn't. If there's anything we can do, just ask. Do you need any money?"

I explained to her what I wanted to do with our possessions. She was hesitant about my not getting my fair share, but I managed to convince her that I didn't want anything more. My father, I knew, wouldn't be so easily convinced; but he would just have to accept it. I asked my mother to explain things to my father, leaving out the extramarital affairs, if she thought it would be possible to avoid telling him. She agreed to do what she could. I hung up the phone, relieved that the conversation had gone as well as it had.

I looked out the front window, and watched as Beth pulled the camper into the driveway. I went and put the dress back on, then went to greet her. By the time I got out there, she had the hood of the truck propped up, and was looking at something with a frown on her face.

"Hi there, stranger."

Beth turned and looked at me, slowly taking in my changed appearance. Finally she said, "I like it, Rita. It's fits you."

"I'm going to wear it tomorrow night to the play at Coaster Theater. I have two tickets, if you'd like to come with me. I think I told you about Jared, the production manager, giving them to me."

"Yes, you did. He's the one Jade has a crush on."

"Right. So would you like to go with me?"

"I'd be delighted."

"Great. Are you interested in getting some lunch any time soon?"

"Actually I just ate, but I'll sit and stare at you in your new dress while you eat."

"Okay. I'll go fix myself something. Let yourself in, when you're done there."

"I'll do that."

I went into the house to scrounge for something for lunch. There didn't seem to be much available, so I went out to see if there was any quiche left from last night's dinner.

When I came out, Beth was just putting the hood of the truck down. "Don't tell me you're done so soon."

"No, I couldn't find anything that appealed to me. I really need to make a big trip to the store. I guess I'm either going to have to take the car, or buy a big red wagon to haul groceries home."

"I kind of like the wagon idea. In the meantime, how about quiche?"

I wrapped my arms around her neck and kissed her. "How's that for a quiche?"

She pulled me back into her arms and planted one on me, "Very nice. Quiche me again."

We laughed, then went into the camper to get the leftovers out of the little refrigerator. I sat down in there to eat it. True to her word, she sat next to me, staring at me while I ate my lunch. When I was finished, she put her hand on my knee. "You look really sexy in this frock, Rita."

"Frock, eh?"

"Frock. And don't say 'Frock you,' or I'll take you at your word and do it right now with all the windows and curtains open."

I looked at her with a mischievous smile.

She stared back at me, her eyes daring me to say it.

"Frock you, you sexy guitar player!"

She slid her hand under the skirt of my dress, and began caressing my thigh. I leaned back in the chair and exhaled slowly. Her other hand joined the first one in there, as though their meeting had been previously arranged. She tried to remove my panties, but couldn't because I was sitting on them. I looked through the open curtains out into the neighborhood, and thought to myself, "Oh well, what the hell. Give them all a thrill. They don't have to look unless they're truly interested."

I raised my rear end off the chair while Beth slid my panties to the floor. She tossed them behind her as I had on the first night we made love. I laughed at her. Her hands moved back into position under my dress, she stuck her head under there too, and began lighting little fires all over my body. She reached up and kneaded my breasts while her mouth explored the softness of my yearning. I was not long in coming, not once, not twice, but three times before I begged her to stop. She came out from under my dress. We were both drenched with sweat.

I asked her again about making love to her, but she still wouldn't let me. She had started cramping again because she had become so aroused from making love to me.

"Damn it. I want you so badly, Beth."

"You'll have your chance."

I thought to myself, *Before you leave, I hope.*

I invited her in for a shower. She accepted, and graciously offered to be my sponge. I had never showered with anyone before, but knowing Beth, I decided it would be a treat I'd not soon forget. I was right.

After our shower, we went for a walk on the beach. The sun was shining, and there was only a light breeze. It was another perfect afternoon. We stopped to talk to a woman who was throwing a Frisbee to her dog. We suspected that she was lesbian, though we didn't inquire. She was visiting from eastern Oregon. I told her about the new play that was opening, and encouraged her to attend. Then we walked on up the beach. We stopped just below Ecola Park. I stood looking out at the Tillamook lighthouse.

Mostly thinking aloud, I said, "Sometimes I wonder what it must've been like to live out there."

"Noisy, I imagine, with the waves pounding the base of the rock."

"Perhaps, but I think that would eventually turn into white noise, the way a fan does, or the sound of a dishwasher."

"Do you think you would like to live in that much solitude?"

"I don't know. Perhaps. I like solitude, but I also like to be around people sometimes. What about you, Beth? Would that be a good place to listen to your heart?"

"I rather think it would. There certainly wouldn't be a lot of distractions."

"I'd probably do a lot of whale watching."

Beth nodded. "It sure is beautiful here. I can see why you want to live here all the time."

I wanted to say, "Then why don't you stay and live here too?" But I was afraid it might spoil the moment, so I refrained. Instead I just said, "I love you, Beth."

She took my hand, and we walked back down the beach to the house. As we walked, I thought about the play

Beth had agreed to attend with me. That let me know that I had at least one more day with her. "What do you think you'll wear to the play?"

"Me? Probably whatever I happen to pick out in the morning. I don't have a large wardrobe. I hope you won't be ashamed to be seen with me."

"I could never be ashamed to be with you."

"I hope not, but I know those things are important to you."

"Probably not as important as you think. I'm just in the middle of a change of image. I'm throwing off the 'Paul's wife' look, and just beginning to discover my new 'Rita, permanent beachcomber' look."

"Well, I really like your new image. It fits the Rita that's inside better."

"Good, I'm glad you feel that way. It feels right to me."

We finished our walk, and headed up the stairs to the house. "Would you like to have dinner in?"

"Why don't I take you somewhere special tonight? You can wear your new dress."

"I think I'd like to save that for Friday evening, but I can wear the outfit I picked out the other day for job-hunting."

"Okay then. Where to?"

"How about the Wayfarer?"

"Fine. Shall I pick you up at 7:00?"

"Pick me up?"

"In the figurative sense, of course. I assume we'll just walk. That's one of the things I'm beginning to like about Cannon Beach. You don't really need to have a car to get around. Everything is so close together."

"Yes, close together." I said, while I was thinking, *the way I want you and me to be.* I held my tongue, an activity I was wearying of quickly.

"Seven is fine. See you then, unless you want to come into the house."

"I'm kind of tired. If I come in, would you mind if I took a nap? I think my cramps are wearing me out."

"You may have your choice of beds. Well, except for the king, since it's in pieces."

"And all the king's horses, and all the king's men, couldn't put Humpty Dumpty's bed back together again. How very sad."

"You nut!"

When we went into the house, I noticed there was a message on the answering machine. It was from my father. He sounded concerned and supportive, but I could tell he wasn't happy about my not fighting for what was due me from the marriage. I wondered how many times I would have to defend my right to be satisfied with what I had. I opted to lie down with Beth in the queen-sized bed. I got a heating pad for her aching belly, then held her while we slept.

Chapter Seventeen

We slept longer than we had planned. Beth woke up cramping, so we decided to have Fultano's deliver one of their delicious pizzas. We spent the evening chatting about books we had read, and been influenced by. Beth's favorite was the *Tao Te Ching*. Mine was Elizabeth Berg's *Pull of the Moon*. It had probably started the wheels turning in my head, long before I met Beth, and long before I realized what a disaster my marriage was.

I showed her my new journal, and let her read what I had written so far. She laughed at my account of the meeting with Emily at the grocery store. "That was pretty funny," Beth said. "The woman obviously didn't major in social subtleties."

"The funny thing is that I had no clue she was lesbian until she saw us, and her mouth hit the ground. I don't know why I didn't see it at first. It seems obvious to me now. I guess I really am heterosexist."

"I hope we've changed that by now to 'were heterosexist.' Please tell me you are no longer of the opinion that heterosexuality is all that exists, or that it's the best thing on earth for everyone."

"Okay, I used to be heterosexist. I think part of my problem is that I'm used to associating primarily with married couples. I'm just not used to thinking about people in terms of their sexual orientation. When you are married, and hang around married couples, you just assume everyone is heterosexual, unless it comes out clearly otherwise."

"And yet according to a lot of the sex studies, a lot more people are bisexual than you would think."

"I wonder if that's what I am."

"What? Bisexual? I don't know. I guess that's one of the things you're going to have to find out about the new Rita."

"I can't say that I've ever felt sexually attracted to a man. At least not the way I feel towards you."

"When did you realize you were attracted to me?"

"Now that's a tough question. I was attracted to you when I first saw you on the beach playing your guitar. But when I first realized what kind of attraction I was experiencing, it was some time in the middle of that first long night of talking."

"That must've been a shock to your system, what with having been married for fifteen years."

"In a way. But in another way, it was very freeing to realize that I could feel so much sexual desire for another person. I guess it's like I'd lived my whole life thinking that there was only vanilla ice cream to eat, and you either liked vanilla, or you didn't."

"And then one day you walked into Baskin-Robbins?"

"That's it exactly! I suddenly realized I had choices. As you can see, it didn't take me long to decide that I wanted something other than vanilla."

"Lucky for me. But, you know, you're making me awfully hungry for ice cream. Are you too full to go make a raid on the yogurt place?"

"Is it still open?"

"I'm not sure, but if not, the grocery store is. I'm

certain they can oblige us. What do you say? I'm on a munch. I think it's because of my period. I always get hungrier than usual."

"Yogurt sounds great to me. I'll grab my jacket."

"I think I will too. It's sounds as though it's getting windy out there."

I went and grabbed my jacket, while Beth went out to the camper. She came out with a flannel shirt instead of a jacket. I found myself getting very fond of flannel and denim. We walked down to the grocery store, and brought home a container of chocolate almond swirl frozen yogurt. We sat on the couch eating it, with our teeth chattering, until I finally got up and built a small fire in the fireplace. Once the fire had warmed our bones, we decided to go to bed. In spite of our nap, we were both sleepy again. Beth stayed and slept with me, instead of going out to the camper.

The next day I called around trying to find a charity that would take Paul's bed. I didn't want to bother with selling it. No one seemed to want to pick it up for a week, so Beth and I carried it out to the garage for temporary storage. Shortly after noon, UPS showed up with two big boxes addressed to me. I signed for them, and had the man set them just inside the front door.

I knew they had to contain my clothes. So I opened them, and starting sorting through what I wished to keep, and what I wanted to discard. I filled the largest box with the discards, then put the other box in my bedroom to be dealt with later. Beth spent the whole day with me, helping me sort through my clothes, rearranging things, and doing general housework.

As evening neared, we parted company in order to get dressed for the play. I put on my lovely new dress. Beth put on a blue and white striped button-down oxford shirt with navy slacks and a matching navy blazer. I was stunned, though I tried not to show it.

"You didn't think I owned anything but jeans, T-shirts, and flannel shirts, did you?"

I didn't say anything.

"Surprised you, huh?"

I nodded, then kissed her. "You look quite sharp."

"Be careful then, you might cut yourself."

I thought, but didn't say, *I'm already bleeding, Beth.*

We had a great time at the play. They were doing *Deathtrap,* one of my favorite plays. After an astounding performance, we went out to mingle in the lobby. We ran into everyone I knew in town--Jade, Emily, Jared, and even the woman we'd met on the beach earlier that day. They all admired my dress. I showed off Jade's handiwork, and heaped praise on her until she blushed. By the time I was finished, I noticed that even Jared was viewing her in a different light.

I caught Emily eyeing Beth again, though less blatantly. I introduced Beth to Jade and Jared as my date. Emily coughed, and took a step back. Beth put an arm around my shoulder, and squeezed me. She leaned over and whispered in my ear, "In case you hadn't noticed, I'm peeing on you, so Emily will get the message."

I smiled and squeezed her back. As we were about to leave, Stacey, the woman from the art gallery, grabbed me by the arm.

"Rita! You look adorable in that dress. It is so, so you! Frederick is back, so we will talk this week, yes?"

"I'd love to."

"Oh, here is Frederick now. I'll introduce you."

Introductions were made all around. No one seemed to mind that I was with a woman. No one even blinked, in fact. Frederick seemed to be enthusiastic about having me come and talk to them about working at the gallery. We made plans for me to stop by the shop on the following Monday morning.

After everyone had dispersed, Beth and I slowly walked home. I could tell there was something troubling Beth, so I tried to get her to talk. She was hesitant, at first, but then she finally let me know that she would be leaving some time that weekend. I was proud of myself. I didn't even cry. It hurt too much to cry and besides, there would be time enough for that later.

She spent the night with me that night and the next. We made love a lot, and spent hours just sitting on beach, listening to the ocean. On Sunday morning, she lifted her anchor, and sailed away in her camper, taking my heart with her. Before she left she gave me the piece of driftwood she had found on the beach. I was instructed to stroke it regularly, and tell it stories about my daily life. When she returned, she would take it back, and listen to all the tales it had to tell until she got caught up on my life.

That night I placed the piece of driftwood on my mantle, and faithfully took it down every evening while she was away. I sat in my bentwood rocker, rocking and stroking, while I told it all about the exciting work I was doing at the gallery. I went to work for Frederick and Stacey, shortly after Beth left. I learned a lot from them, and really enjoyed the work. So much so, I eventually decided that I would like to open my own shop in town.

As I sat and rocked, I told the wood about Jade and her masterpieces. Not only did I get Jade to design a new wardrobe for me, I also commissioned her to start supplying me with dresses and outfits to sell in the shop I planned to open. Eventually she quit working at the bookstore to devote more time and energy to designing.

I told the wood about Emily trying to seduce me, some three months after Beth had gone. She called one evening to ask if she could stop by for a drink. I didn't know quite how to get out of it, so I agreed to let her come over. As the evening wore on, it was obvious that she wanted to console me about Beth's absence, by filling the void with her own presence. I politely declined, while assuaging her ego with the diplomatic elegance in which I had been so well versed. Somehow she managed to get the message without becoming obviously annoyed about it.

I told the driftwood everything from local gossip to world news, hoping as I did so that Beth would really come back some day to reclaim both it and me. It was true that I was lonely without her, yet I continued to grow in my newfound sense of independence.   During her absence, I realized that I could live without Beth, but that I preferred to live with her.   I realized too that there could never be another person who could take her place in my life.

I frequently played the tape I had made of her music. I played it so often I was afraid the tape would wear out, so I made another copy of it. I memorized the words to all the songs, and I sang them with her, eyes closed, pretending that she was there in the room with me. When I took walks on the beach, I imagined her sitting there on the log, just as she had been when I first encountered her. Sometimes I could almost hear her singing, as though the waves were slowly echoing back her serenade.

When she left she had promised to call occasionally, and she did. Once a month I would get a call from her. The first time she called from eastern Oregon. She had been following the Oregon Trail. Another time she called from Bandon on the southern coast of Oregon. She had just finished taking a photographic tour of Oregon lighthouses. She sent me a postcard at each stop along the way. Another time she called from Fort Stevens, just north of Cannon Beach. I found it intriguing that the woman who loved to travel, far and wide, never left the state. Her wanderings were beginning to look as though they were spiraling her back to me.

During our phone conversations, I refrained from telling her much about my daily life, since that was the purpose of the driftwood. What I did share with her were the many antics of the two kittens I had gotten from the people at the campground. I had named the gray fluff ball Dustin, for he looked like a dust bunny. The white one I had named Nik, which was short for Beatnik, since his little goatee made him look like one. They pulled so many hilarious stunts in their early months with me that I often accused Beth of purposefully going away to avoid their mischievous kittenhood. Yet, in spite of all their misdeeds, they were a great solace to me while Beth was away.

When she unexpectedly showed up at my front door six months after she'd left, she had a compact disc of her music in her hand. She had met someone in Portland who owned a music studio. In exchange for some carpentry work, she had been granted access to a recording studio and a sound technician. The result was phenomenal. The recording did justice to her talent, and soon after she returned, the album was selling in many of the local shops.

Within a year of my moving to Cannon Beach, I was able, with financial backing from my parents, to open the "Spiraling Driftwood." So as not to compete too much with the existing galleries, we concentrated on avant-garde clothing, furniture, and jewelry. Of course, we also sold Beth's music, a collection that eventually included five albums. In order to promote Beth's music, we turned the shop into a sort of coffeehouse once a month, so she could perform her songs locally. She also occasionally ventured to nearby towns for other performances.

After her return, Beth became my partner in love as well as my partner in work. She was finally able to settle into a job she liked that also allowed her the time she needed to work on her music. We went on many trips together over the years, including to Western Europe and the Mediterranean. Jade, who worked for us part-time, ran the store in our absence.

While I can't say so for certain, I don't think Beth ever again felt the need to drift off on her own. That is, until she drifted away from me for the last time. After six years of living and loving together, she drifted out onto the sea of eternity. A lifetime of listening to her heartbeat ended when her heart gave out one day after a vigorous walk on the beach. I had not known she had a weak heart until the day of her heart attack. I never found out if she had been aware of it, or if that had been what made her live life so circumspectly. Somehow, I suspect, she must've known her heartbeats were numbered, and during the time I knew her, I don't think she wasted a single one of them.

I never did join the theater group. I got too involved with the art gallery, and later with my own shop.

After Beth died, I turned over management to a young couple from Texas. A young lesbian couple, that is. I later sold the business to them, and retired from the art business, and from the world in general. Without Beth to enjoy it with me, my work just wasn't as fulfilling as it had been. But I found that being a recluse fit the grief stricken Rita quite well.

So now I sit here remembering our years together. They were fun years, happy years, filled with early morning walks along the beach and exquisitely poetic lovemaking. Although my years with Beth were few, I wouldn't trade them for anything else in the world. While I can no longer hold Beth's body in my arms at night, I will always hold the memory of her beautiful face in my heart. I took a photograph of her playing in the grass with the cats. The sun is glinting off her hair revealing its rich indigo highlights. That photo still graces my nightstand; the lingering memory of her touch still fills my dreams.

Her guitar resides in the corner of the living room that is nearest to the dining room. It seems almost as though she will come in at any moment, pick it up, and start playing me a love song. She wrote a song once about how her presence would never leave me, and how even when I could not see her, she would be right there with me. I think she has kept that promise.

Sometimes when I open the window to listen to the sound of the waves, the ocean breeze floats in and sets the guitar strings to humming, ever so slightly. I catch my breath whenever that happens, as I feel her presence strongest then. I suspect that the cats might be able to see her. For whenever that happens, their fur stands on end, and they stop and stare at the guitar as though it has just come alive. Sometimes Dustin will venture up to the guitar and rub against it as though it is Beth herself.

I don't know what I would do without the constant companionship of the cats. They've sat with me through many days and nights, listening to me talking about Beth while I stroke my little piece of driftwood. They sleep with me every night in the queen-sized futon I purchased shortly after I left Paul. Without Dustin and Nik, I don't think I could've have made it through those first months during Beth's absence. I know I couldn't have survived without them during those first days and weeks after Beth died.

As for my former husband, I haven't seen him since the divorce was final. He didn't fight me. His lawyer advised him not to, since I wasn't asking for much. Yet I got the only thing I wanted from our marriage—my house by the sea. I have never regretted not asking for more than that. I didn't need anything else, though I received a great deal more.

My friendship with Jade continues, albeit from a distance. Several years ago, she met a man on the beach who was visiting from Australia. They fell in love, and he continues to treat her as the precious gem she is. She is still designing clothes, though now she lives in Sydney, and has two children.

Emily has had a series of female lovers. None of her relationships seems to last very long. We are civil when we see each other in town, which isn't often, thankfully. I cannot truly call her a friend. I never felt as though I could trust her, and she seemed to hate Beth because she had stolen my heart.

My cottage in Cannon Beach continues to be my haven of refuge. It's where I hide from the world. It's where I feel closest to nature, and to Beth. It's the one place where I can always count on being able to hear my heartbeat.

Beth's little piece of driftwood still sits on my mantle. I continue to stroke it daily, telling it how much I miss her, and our life together. The wood has been stroked so many times that I fear it will break in two one day. It has worn thin in places, through the telling and retelling of this story. I sometimes wonder if it will remain in tact until I drift away at last to rejoin Beth. I swear sometimes I can hear her singing, even when the stereo is off. I stroke the wood in time to her music, to the last song she ever wrote for me:

When the sun comes up in the morning
When the moon is high at night
When the flowers bloom in the springtime
Then will I be here

When the sun shines down on the garden
When the moon is full and bright
When the rains pour down in the summer
Then will I be here

I will be here, ever and ever
I will be here through the years
Even when you cannot see me
I will be right here

When the sun goes to bed in the evening
When the moon hides behind the clouds
When the leaves fall down in the autumn
Then will I be here

When the sun moves away from the mountains
When the moon can't be seen at night
When the snowfall comes in the winter
Then will I be here

I will be here ever and ever
I will be here through the years
Even when you cannot see me
I will be right here
Even when you cannot see me
I will be right here.

About the Author

Beth Mitchum was raised in central Florida. She attended college there then went to work in a children's home, where she cared for abused teens for over four years. She moved to western North Carolina in 1985, where she was able to pursue her love of nature and the outdoors. While there, she earned a Masters degree in humanities, a broad field of liberal arts studies, which she continues to pursue on her own. She has spent nearly all her life engaging in creative endeavors.

After teaching herself to play the guitar at age twelve, she began writing songs the following year. With an active imagination from an early age, it's no surprise that she has turned into a writer of books as well. She recalls writing whole new episodes in her head of her favorite television shows. She would then act them out by herself, complete with the dialog for all the characters involved. Thus, it was clear that she was destined either to become a writer of some sort or a victim of multiple personality disorder. So far, the former seems to be the case. Having moved to western Washington in 1993 .

Sparks Might Fly
by Cris Newport

Excerpt from Chapter One

Pip struggled up from the grey dampness of sleep. The room, fully dark, seemed less real than her dream. This was not the first time she'd wandered a long-remembered dream-road through curving hillsides, past dark windowed cottages toward the grey promise of dawn. But it never came. For many nights she had wandered this road, angling toward the light, while leafless trees, twisted and gnarled, stood in mute witness, and ground fog muffled her steps.

The dream image sharpened and clarified as she came fully awake. Long ago, when she'd read Dickens' *Great Expectations*, she'd been taken by the hero's mist enshrouded departure from his boyhood home. But the fictional Pip's way had been clearer and the mists had risen as his coach sped toward London and the fulfillment of his destiny. Her way was cluttered with old ghosts and obscuring fog. This dream-road seemed to have no beginning and no end. There was only this middle-track and in all the nights of this dreaming, she never rounded the final corner to face what lay ahead.

Pip knew what she would find, even though she always woke before she saw it: Corrinne and Linda entwined together among damp leaves and grasses. Corrinne's eyes would be half-closed in pleasure, her body reclining under Linda's touch. And she would look at Pip curiously and say, "Don't you get it, Pip? It's over. Go home."

Pip dressed quietly and slipped downstairs. Opening the french doors, she stepped outside. It was deliciously cool and the sky was pearl colored. A brief respite from the stifling heat. She walked toward the pines. . . .

She strode through the dewy grass, feeling the gentle roll of the land under her feet as it sloped down toward the woods. The dream images faded slowly. She sat on the stump of an old tree and looked back toward the house. It was dark and quiet. Although she did not want to remember, she could not stop the memories of Corrinne.

Corrinne's face was still as clear to her as it had been a year ago. She could recall every expression, every movement from her whimsical, seductive gaze to the cold harshness that had come later. From the sultry swing of her narrow hips to the rigid way she'd clasped and unclasped her hands during their final confrontation. Pip had seen dark circles under Corrinne's eyes, partially hidden by sun browned skin, eyes framed by just the barest hint of lashes, eyes that sometimes seemed too small for her face.

Pip remembered the way her breasts strained against her bra; how broad her shoulders were, how narrow her hips. When they'd first met, Corrinne had been solid, with a rounded belly and a wide flat behind that seemed out of place with her coltish legs and slender arms. Corrinne's body was a warm resting place with curved softness and bony edges, a striking contrast to her alternately seductive and manipulative personality. While Corrinne longed for closeness, for connection, Pip knew she feared it more than anything else. And while Pip offered her a vision of a home, a life, a future, it was not the same vision Corrinne held. They had talked of raising children, of living together and Pip hung her hopes on those dreams, not realizing they were insubstantial as mist.

Pip entered the large reception room and was immediately surrounded. Someone shoved a glass of champagne into her hand, a rough voice called out a toast. It was another opening night in London. A sold out crowd, most of whom, Pip noted with a measure of distaste, seemed to have been invited to the reception. She nodded and smiled and sipped her champagne. She was overwhelmed by the smells of mingling perfumes, sweat and aftershave.

Pip caught her manager's eye over the head of an old man who was enthusiastically raving about her performance. Susan mouthed, "Forty-five," and Pip nodded wearily. Another public relations game — forty-five minutes with the crowd.

Susan Jansen had been with Pip for three and a half years. During the first two years of Pip's professional career, which began in 1985, the Van Cliburn Foundation provided a manager. When that commitment ended, the Foundation recommended Susan, who had been in the business for over ten years. Now, at forty-eight, Susan looked closer to thirty-five and boasted a vast reserve of patience and energy — both of which were unspoken prerequisites for this type of job.

Susan was also Pip's confidant and friend, although to hear Pip shouting at her at times would belie that fact. Susan tolerated Pip's moods. It was something else they both knew went with the territory. She mingled easily with the patrons, more easily than Pip could manage, her slender body moving in easy, unforced, conversational comradery. Pip envied her sometimes and the calming effect she had on others. For Pip, this kind of socializing was sheer torture. Forty-five minutes later, Pip excused herself and retreated to the balcony.

She slipped into the shadows and leaned on the stone railing. In the distance, the city lights flickered. The cold January air was refreshing after the close stuffiness of the reception hall and Pip wished to be anywhere but where she was. She was not quite half-way through a tour that would end in August, then Pip would have a few weeks off before beginning another. A never ending cycle. And, as usual, at this point on the curve of the touring circle, she was looking forward to nothing more than rest and solitude. The company of strangers, no matter how enthusiastic, was numbing.

She felt someone join her and sighed. Not wishing to acknowledge this new person, she didn't move, but pretended she hadn't heard the scrape of leather on the stone or smelled the slightly soapy scent of the woman's perfume.

She still didn't turn when the woman leaned on the railing

next to her, facing in toward the reception. Pip waited for her to speak and when she did, Pip turned and saw Corrinne for the first time. "These events are an incredible bore sometimes, don't you think?"

"I guess it depends on your point of view," Pip said, remembering a time when she'd said just that to the wife of the host and regretted it long after.

"My lover practically insists I attend opening nights, but I'd prefer to stay home with a volume of Emily Dickinson and a roaring fire."

Pip smiled. "That sounds lovely."

Corrinne slipped suddenly into the shadows, pressing up against Pip. Startled, Pip pulled back but Corrinne said, "There she goes now. I just wanted a moment's peace from her possessiveness." She pointed to a small woman in a black evening dress. Pip recognized her. It was Margaret, the tympani player for the symphony.

"That's your lover?"

"You sound surprised."

"It's a bit of a relief to meet a woman open about her preferences."

"And you? Are you open about your preferences?"

"It depends what part of the world I'm in."

Corrinne raised one slender eyebrow and smiled in acknowledgement. "Forgive me, I should have introduced myself. Corrinne Leger."

Pip noted that she pronounced her last name with a decidedly French accent. "Pip Martin."

"I know."

"I figured."

"Will you be in London long?"

"A few days. Then up to Edinburgh, across to Dublin. Back to Paris, then... it's quite endless, really." She was bored and glanced back into the reception area looking for Susan.

"And do you have any free time during your stay in our wonderful city?"

Pip thought for a moment. "Not really. Except for a few hours in the morning, I have rehearsals and then performances. But I'll be in Edinburgh for two weeks, enough time for a short vacation." Pip rubbed absently at the back of her neck trying to ease the tension caught there.

"Let me," Corrinne said. She moved behind Pip and began expertly massaging her neck. "Take off your jacket."

Pip complied. She could feel the tension easing. "You're good."

"I should be. I do this for a living."

"Can I interest you in employment? I'm in desperate need of a decent massage."

"I'd be honored. Where and when?"

Corrinne dropped her hands and Pip turned to face her. Her headache had diminished significantly.

She looked at her watch. "The Prince Hotel, room 712. One hour."

Corrinne looked a bit surprised, but then she smiled. "All right." She seemed just about to say something else when Margaret swept onto the balcony, looking frazzled but trying to appear casual.

"There you are," Margaret said. "I've been looking for you everywhere."

"I'm right here, darling," Corrinne said in a voice edged with displeasure.

"I see you've met Phillipa," Margaret stumbled on.

Pip nodded.

"Well," Margaret said into the silence, "we really should be going."

"So soon?" Corrinne asked. "But we only just got here."

"Yes, but it's a long cab ride home and I'm quite exhausted."

"You go on," Corrinne said. "Phillipa has asked me to join her later."

Margaret's eyes widened and Corrinne said with a tight smile, "Professional reasons, my dear. Let me walk you down to the cab stand." She turned to Pip. "It was nice meeting you." She extended her hand. Pip took it, felt a flush of embarrassment spread over her as Corrinne held her hand longer than was necessary. She trailed her fingertips across Pip's palm as she let go and Pip felt a pang of desire. "I'll see you in an hour."

"Yes." Pip's eyes flitted to Margaret's face, registered the fear and anxiety there. Margaret tried to steer Corrinne away, but Corrinne extricated herself skillfully from the touch and led the way back into the reception hall. Margaret followed after, shoulders slumped in defeat.

Pip watched them for a moment, then pushed her way back into the party. She saw Susan talking with the Symphony conductor and caught her eye. A moment later Susan excused herself and joined Pip on the balcony. "I'm leaving."

Susan glanced at her watch.

"You said forty-five minutes. It's been over an hour."

"Yes. But I didn't mean for you to spend the entire time out here flirting with Margaret's girlfriend."

Pip waved her hand dismissively. "I didn't. I spent exactly forty-five minutes in the reception room. *Then* I was flirting with Margaret's girlfriend."

"Pip, be careful. You still have to work with these people. You know your flirtations sometimes backfire. You do tend to make this difficult for those of us trying to help you."

"Help me? Help me do what? All I have to do is show up and play."

"Yes. That's all you have to do. But I have to make all the arrangements."

"Oh, Christ, Susan. Lighten up."

"Pip, please. Leave Margaret alone."

"I have no intention of touching Margaret. Her so-called girlfriend is a masseuse and she's meeting me at the hotel in an hour. Don't wake me up until eleven tomorrow."

"The rehearsal's at eleven thirty."

"I'll be ready. I'm always ready, Susan. You know that. Have I ever missed a rehearsal?"

"No."

"A performance?"

"No."

"Have I even been even one minute late for anything?"

"No, Pip. "

"I rest my case. Now, get some sleep. I'll see you in the morning." Pip put her jacket back on and walked away, ignoring the feeling of Susan's eyes boring into her back. She worries too much, Pip thought. Then she dismissed it and thought instead of how she would get Corrinne into her bed.

Corrinne Leger arrived on time. A point in her favor; Pip detested anyone who was late. She carried a black bag over her left shoulder and a large square object wrapped in a protective cover. She smiled when Pip let her into the hotel suite.

"What's that?" Pip asked, gesturing.

"That's my table. Can't work without it." She tossed her bag onto the floor and unzipped the table's cover. A few minutes later, she'd set it up in the middle of the floor. She threw a clean white sheet from her bag over the top and a blanket over that. "If you'll get ready, I'll be back in a minute."

Pip nodded and while Corrinne went into the bathroom, she stripped off her clothes and slid between sheet and blanket. A moment later, Corrinne returned. She set out a series of bottles on the floor near her feet and began to work.

Corrinne clearly knew what she was doing. Her fingers were deft and strong and they kneaded into the knotted muscles as though she'd been working on Pip for years. Pip felt herself relaxing and her mind drifted toward seduction. She said, "How long have you been seeing Margaret?"

"About four months. But she's too possessive for me. I feel as though I have to report in every time I take a shit."

"What's the draw then?"

"Oh, she's stable, Pip. And I liked that, especially in the beginning. I can depend on her to be very consistent in her moods and attitudes. She's a rock and I'm water. Sometimes that's nice. But nice only goes so far and I'm getting tired of feeling like I'm chained to that rock."

"What was it about her that made you want her initially?"

"You ask a lot of personal questions."

"Are you going to answer it?"

Corrinne laughed and her fingers probed deeper into the tense muscles of Pip's shoulder. Pip grunted. "She's one hell of a musician. She has a set of African drums at her house and when she plays them, I feel as though my body will just fly apart. It's as though the rhythms just pound right through me. I love it. I guess I've always had a weakness for musicians. I just like to imagine how their hands will feel on my body."

"Oh?"

"Oh, yourself. Now, just relax Ms. Martin. You're thinking too much."

Pip laughed softly and gave herself over to Corrinne's hands. . . . . Convinced the entire massage was merely a prelude to lovemaking, as Pip rose from the table and slipped on her robe, she was already imagining what it would be like.

Corrinne returned from the bathroom. Pip walked toward her, smiling slightly. "You'll stay, of course."

Corrinne blushed. "I'm sorry, Pip. I can't."

Confused and startled, Pip took a step backward. "Have to report in?" she sneered.

"No. But I am tired. Perhaps I could have a rain check?"

"Perhaps," Pip's voice was cold as she tried to cover her embarrassment. It had been a long time since she had been refused.

Corrinne picked up her belongings and headed for the door. "I hope I'll see you again."

"Yes," Pip said, not sure whether she meant it or not.

One week later, after the first of three consecutive performances in Edinburgh, someone knocked on Pip's dressing room door. When Pip opened it, she was surprised to find Corrinne standing there. "What are you doing here?" Pip asked.

"I came to see you." Corrinne sat down in a battered overstuffed chair and crossed one leg demurely over the other. She wore a black skirt of raw silk that fell to mid-calf over a dark green body suit that accentuated her full breasts. Her foot bobbed up and down with barely contained energy. She swept her dark hair back from her face and smiled.

Pip leaned against the dressing table and crossed her arms over her chest. Corrinne got up and stood before her. Pip studied her face. Her skin was scarred under her chin and around her mouth from a losing battle with acne. Her lips were full, her eyes small and dark. She smiled and raised her hands to Pip's face. Pip pulled away. "Feeling more rested tonight?"

"Perhaps."

"How about a nightcap then?" Corrinne nodded. Pip swung her black greatcoat over her shoulders and gestured for Corrinne to precede her out the door. In the hotel bar, Pip guided them to a secluded booth and ordered two snifters of brandy. Cupping hers between her hands, Pip let the warmth from her palms release the fragrances from the liquor. She looked at Corrinne over the top of her glass. "I'm surprised to see you here," she said.

"Why?"

"When you left last week you acted as though it was strictly a business deal."

"Last week, it was. Tonight is another story."

"Oh?" Pip raised her eyebrows. "And how's that?"

"You're performance tonight was stunning."

"You're changing the subject," Pip said.

"Actually," Corrinne smiled slowly, "I'm not."

Pip sipped her brandy. "I see."

"Do you?"

Pip nodded. "Yes." She drained her glass. "Tomorrow night I'm playing Liszt. Come see me after the performance." She touched Corrinne's hand where it rested on the table. "Watch my hands. And imagine."

Corrinne shivered. Pip got up abruptly and left the bar.

The second night, they met again in the dressing room. Pip had already changed from her performance outfit into a pair of tight jeans and an oversized linen shirt. She was sipping champagne when Corrinne knocked at the door. She handed Corrinne a glass.

"Do you always play that way?"

"Tonight, I played for you."

Corrinne set her glass down and came into Pip's arms. Pip kissed her hungrily. Her hands pushed up under Corrinne's blouse, felt the lace of her bra under her fingertips. She could feel Corrinne trembling and her own knees were weak.

"I want you now," Pip said.

"Tomorrow night is your last performance here. You said you'll have a few days off," Corrinne said.

"Yes."

"Play for me again tomorrow. Play as if you were touching me with as much passion as you touch those keys. Then tomorrow, after the performance, we'll go back to your hotel room—"

"I don't want to wait."

"But it'll be so powerful. Like magic."

"You love this don't you?" Pip asked.

"What?"

"This game, this chase. Touch and retreat. It turns you on."

"Incredibly."

"All right, then. Tomorrow night."

Corrinne smiled. She kissed Pip again, deeply, achingly. Then she slipped out the door and was gone.

For more information about how to order *Sparks Might Fly*, please see the catalogue information on the following pages.

Other Windstorm Creative Titles
You Might Enjoy

Sparks Might Fly by Cris Newport. Classically trained pianist Pip Martin was a child prodigy. But the disastrous ending to a passionate love affair has made Pip unable to play a single note. Canceling a lucrative European tour, Pip returns to Boston, never suspecting that love will find her there.
ISBN 0-934678-61-8   Price: $9.95

1001 Nights: Exotica by Cris Newport. A multicultural cast highlights this collection of true-life inspired stories of erotic encounters between women. Illustrated with black and white drawings.
ISBN 1-886383-82-0   Price: $12.95

Annabel and I by Chris Anne Wolfe. Annabel's world is of the 1880s and Jenny-wren's the 1980s. The magic of Lake Chautauqua brings them together, bridging two very different worlds. Illustrated with enchanting pen and ink drawings.
ISBN 1886383-17-0   Price: $10.95

Keeper of the Piece by Lesley Davis. A new novel from British writer Davis. Lorrah Gliden is determined to find the fabled Missourose, but the only woman who seems to know where it is wants nothing to do with her — initially. When Lorrah's enthusiasm convinces the reclusive Tate to accompany her into the mountains, the two women embark on a remarkable and romantic journey.
ISBN 1-886383-70-7   Price: $12.95

Queen's Champion: The Legend of Lancelot Retold by Cris Newport. A lyrical and ground-breaking retelling of the classic Arthurian love story. Only in this version, Lancelot is a woman. Illustrated with black and white drawings.
ISBN 1-886383-20-0   Price: $11.95

Roses & Thorns by Chris Anne Wolfe. A beautiful and moving lesbian retelling of *The Beauty and the Beast*. Illustrated in the classic silhouette style.
ISBN 1886383-64-2   Price: $12.95

more ⟶

Long Way Home by Melissa Romero. When Veronica's mother, Maggie, comes out, she packes up her three kids and leaves her marriage. When Veronica's father has Maggie declared unfit, Ronnie is caught between her mother's home filled with love and the verbal and physical abuse she experiences from her father. Ronnie struggles to hold onto what's most precious, coming finally to understand her mother's simple truth: Home is where the heart is.
ISBN 1-883573-15-7   Price: 12.95

And Featuring Bailey Wellcom as the Biscuit by Peggy Durbin. When twelve-year-old Bailey and her mom move to the sleepy town of Lucien, New Mexico, Bailey is sure her life is going to be snoresville. But then they meet cattlewoman Melody Callahan, and things get really interesting, for Bailey *and* her mom!
ISBN 1886383-88-X   Price: $12.95

1000 Reasons You Might Think She is My Lover by Angela Costa. One thousand spicy poems to share with someone you love.
ISBN 1-886383-21-9   Price: $10.95

talking drums by Jan Bevilacqua. A collection of erotic, groundbreaking poems.
ISBN 1-886383-13-8   Price: $9.95

Signs of Love by Leslea Newman. First released in two volumes, this moving collection of poetry chronicles the author's moving journey from childhood to adulthood.
ISBN 1-886383-45-6   Price: $12.95

The Perfect Lesbian Pre-Nuptial Agreement by C.W. Cecil. Want to ensure that his money is your money and your money is your money? Worried that he might stray from the home-sweet-home you envision? Get him to sign on the dotted line ... and you'll never stop laughing.
ISBN 1-886383-87-1   Price: $9.95

Still Life with Buddy by Leslea Newman. A novel told in poetic form about the devout friendship between a lesbian and her best friend who dies of AIDS. Winner of a National Endowment of the Arts award.
ISBN 1-886383-27-8   Price: $9.95

Get a Life! One that Makes You Happy by Linda Dorsett. Looking for your very own Prince Charming? Using the framework of the *Cinderella* story, Dorsett uses practical examples from a wide

variety of cultures and lifestyles to deal with life's most
challenging issues.
ISBN 1-886383-63-4   Price: $10.95

Write and Publish Your Life Story: Guaranteed! by BetteLou
Tobin. Use this book as a guide for writing your autobiography
and Windstorm Creative will publish it. (There is **NO FEE**
charged for publication.)
ISBN 1-886383-61-8   Price: $12.95

Journey of a Thousand Miles by Peter Kasting. Set in a
frightening and believable future, Rafael sets out on an incredible
journey toward self-fulfillment and love. Kasting's dynamic
multi-cultural cast of unique and passionate characters is
unforgettable.
ISBN 1-883573-35-1.   Price: $14.95

How Apollo Stole Pride by Tom French. From the author of the
comic *Apollo's World* comes a hysterically funny spoof on both
Gay Pride merchandising and *How the Grinch Stole Christmas*.
ISBN 1-886383-49-9   Price: $2.95

Visit Windstorm Creative Limited's web site for
more titles at great prices in all genres.
www.windstormcreative.com
Direct purchases receive an automatic
20% discount.

About this Book

The book you're holding is handmade, something quite rare in this day and age. All of Windstorm Creative Limited's titles are printed, bound and trimmed by hand using an environmental-friendly process. Discrepancies in the depth of margins, even with the book, are quite normal. All our books are made to order.

OLD BRIDGE NEAR PETERSBURG.